AF443013

THE GUNSMITH

490

Deadly Debt

Books by J.R. Roberts
(Robert J. Randisi)

The Gunsmith series

Gunsmith Giant series

Lady Gunsmith series

Angel Eyes series

Tracker series

Mountain Jack Pike series

COMING SOON!
The Gunsmith
491 – Invitation to a Bank Robbery

For more information
visit: www.SpeakingVolumes.us

THE GUNSMITH

490

Deadly Debt

J.R. Roberts

SPEAKING VOLUMES, LLC
NAPLES, FLORIDA
2024

Deadly Debt

Copyright © 2024 by Robert J. Randisi

All rights reserved. No part of this book may be reproduced or transmitted in any form or by any means without written permission.

ISBN 979-8-89022-177-3

Chapter One

Clint Adams topped a rise and reined his Tobiano in.

He stared down at a one-story house that was in need of some work. It looked like a ranch that was once a going concern, but had fallen on hard times. Along with the house was a corral, a barn, and a well. While he watched a man came out of the barn, carrying a wooden bucket to the well.

Andy Saxon had sent a telegram to Clint, asking him to meet him here at his ranch on the outskirts of Bent Fork, Oregon. It had taken the message a few weeks to catch up to Clint, and then another week of riding to get there. As he started down the rise Saxon looked up, saw Clint, set the bucket down, and waited.

It was a number of years—three, four, maybe even half-a-dozen—since Clint had last seen Saxon. At that time Saxon had been plying his trade as a hired gun. Since then, from the looks of things, the man's vocation may have changed. He wasn't even wearing a gun.

Saxon leaned against the well while he waited for Clint to reach him. When he did, he greeted him with a relieved smile.

Clint dismounted and approached Saxon with an outstretched hand. Saxon grabbed it and shook it enthusiastically.

"You got my message," Saxon said.

"It caught up to me in Carson City," Clint said.

"Let's take your horse into the barn, and then go to the house."

They unsaddled the Tobiano in the barn, put him in a stall with some feed, and walked to the house. The stairs in front were in need of shoring up, like the rest of the house—heck, the whole ranch.

Inside Saxon said, "Take a load off. Whiskey or coffee?"

"Coffee, Andy." Clint sat at a wobbly table.

Saxon went to the stove and poured two cups, carried them to the table. He set them down and sat across from Clint.

"Your telegram said you had trouble," Clint said. "I have to tell you I might not have even come, except I was headed this way."

"Well, I'm glad you did, whatever the reason," Saxon said. "I got trouble."

"Gun trouble?"

"That's part of it," Saxon said. "I put up my gun, Clint. I promised Mary I wouldn't pick it up, again."

"Mary?"

"The girl I'm gonna get married to when this place is up and runnin'."

"Hitched?" Clint said. "It's been a few years, but I never thought I'd hear that word coming out of your mouth."

"I'm closin' in on forty," Saxon said. "I figure it's time to settle down. When this place came up for sale, I grabbed it."

"So what's the trouble?"

"Seems I grabbed it before somebody else did, and they don't like it."

"Who's that?"

"I don't know," Saxon said. "But whoever it is, they're tryin' to cause me a lot of trouble."

"What kind?"

"Little things at first," Saxon said. "Salt in the well, fire in the bar . . ."

"Yeah, I saw charring in there."

". . . I've got a few cows, and they just happened to wander off."

"Cows do that."

"Then somebody took a shot at me," Saxon said.

"That sounds more serious. Did you go to the law?"

"I did. Sheriff Richards, in Bent Fork."

"What did he do?"

"Not much," Saxon replied. "He said he 'looked into it and didn't find nothin'.'"

"And that's when you sent for me?"

"I need help, and you're the one I thought of."

"Strap on your gun and handle it yourself, Andy," Clint suggested.

"I can't," Saxon said. "I swore to Mary no more gun play."

"Does she know what's going on?" Clint asked.

"She does," Saxon said. "That was why I went to the law."

"What does she want you to do?" Clint asked.

"Leave it to the law," Saxon said, "or sell the place."

"Is she willing to marry you without it?" Clint asked.

"She is, but I'm not givin' this place up," Saxon said.

"It's not much, Andy. You can probably find something better."

"Until somebody tries to make me sell that one," Saxon said.

"Not if you're wearing a gun."

"I told you, I can't do that."

"Andy, you know what happens when somebody like you or me takes their gun off."

"I gave 'er my word, Clint."

"So you want me to make your gun play for you."

"You're the best, Clint."

"But I don't hire my gun out."

"I'm not askin' to hire you, Clint," Saxon said, "I'm askin' for a favor."

Clint had gotten requests for favors like this before, and they usually did lead to gun play. He was tired of it. Not tired enough to take off his gun, like Andy Saxon, but enough to start saying no.

"I can't do it, Andy," Clint said.

"You're refusin' to help me?"

"I'd help anybody who couldn't help themselves," Clint said, "but you're capable."

"I told you why I can't do it."

Clint stood up.

"You're letting a woman call the play, Andy," he said. "I'm not willing to do that. Plus it could take weeks. I can't stay."

"You got something that important to do?"

"I owe somebody else a favor, and that's where I was headed," Clint said. "I'll tell you what I'll do. I'll stop here on my way back, and see how things are going. That's enough time for you to get this place up and running. Maybe I'll even be here in time for the wedding."

"You know what?" Saxon said. "You ain't invited!"

Chapter Two

Evanston, Wyoming
One month later . . .

Clint turned over in bed and stared at Sylvia Haley's beautiful back and butt. A woman of forty, she had the body of a thirty-year-old. He had met her a few years ago, and was surprised to hear from her, asking for help. She bought a ranch and needed help getting it set up. Hiring hands and a foreman. It had taken about two weeks, but things were looking good and he was ready to move on.

She stirred, rolled over and looked at him. Her peach-sized breasts sagged only slightly to each side, then she covered her face with her hands.

"I look terrible," she said, from behind her hands.

"You look just as beautiful as you do every morning," he told her.

"You're such a good liar," she said, looking out from between her fingers. Then she sat up, dropped her hands, leaned back against the headboard and pulled the sheet up to cover her breasts.

"Are you still leaving today?"

"Yes.

"To go where?"

"I told a friend I'd drop in on him when I finished here," he said.

"So he's waiting for you?"

"I doubt it," Clint said. "He was pretty mad at me last time I saw him."

"Why?"

"He has his reasons," Clint said.

"Well," she said, easing over to him, "let's say good-bye in a memorable way."

She came into his arms, pressing her breasts against his chest. He kissed her, long and hard, running his hands over her glorious body. She lifted one leg over him, came into his lap with his penis trapped between them. She rubbed her wet pussy over him, and when he was soaked in her fluids, took him inside. She started to bounce up and down on his rigid cock, and he matched her rhythm. Before long they were both breathing hard until, finally, he exploded inside her . . .

***

She watched him get dressed and strap on his gun.

"Are you going to get dressed?" Clint asked.

"No," she said. "We said goodbye, already. I don't want to watch you ride away."

"I understand."

"I hope your friend's not too angry with you when you get there."

"We'll see."

He bent, kissed her, and left.

***

Outside he ran into Randy Davis, the foreman he had hired to run Sylvia's ranch. He was holding the reins of Clint's Tobiano.

"I thought you'd be needin' this," the man said.

"Thanks." Clint took the reins from him.

"I wanna thank you for takin' me on," Davis said.

"I know you'll do a good job for Sylvia," Clint said. "And keep the men in line."

"They're a good bunch," Davis said. "I think she'll do real well with this ranch."

"I won't be back," Clint said. "I'm leaving the place, and Sylvia, in your hands."

"I understand," Davis said. "Good luck to you, wherever you go next."

Clint gave the man a salute and rode off.

Chapter Three

Bent Fork, Oregon
Two weeks later . . .

When Clint topped the familiar rise outside Andy Saxon's ranch and looked down, he saw something completely unfamiliar. During the time he was gone, Saxon seemed to have totally transformed the place. The buildings had been repaired, the grounds upgraded, the corral was filled with horses. The place looked like a going concern.

He rode down and approached the house, with several hands stopping what they were doing to watch. One man came over and stood by his Tobiano.

"Can I help you?" the man asked. "I'm the foreman here, Tom Finn."

Finn was a big man in his forties. He looked formidable, even though he wasn't wearing a gun.

"I'm looking for Andy Saxon," Clint said. "He owns this place."

"You better talk to Mr. Maitland," Finn said. "I'll get 'im."

He mounted the steps and entered the house, returning moments later with a white-haired man in his sixties.

"I'm Frank Maitland. You lookin' for Saxon?" he asked.

"I am."

"Who're you?"

"My name's Clint Adams. Andy's a friend of mine."

"Well," Maitland said, "I bought this ranch from Andy about a month ago."

"I was here about six or eight weeks back," Clint said. "You've done quite a job with this place."

"Thanks," Maitland said. "I saw the potential here."

"Do you know where Andy went after he sold it?" Clint asked.

"You'll find Saxon in Bent Fork," Finn said.

"We've got work to do," Maitland said. "We can't waste any more time. Sorry."

"That's okay," Clint said. "Thank you."

Clint turned his Tobiano and rode off in the direction of Bent Fork.

***

He rode about five miles before He came to a sign that said BENT FORK Pop. 1504. He had no idea Bent Fork was that large. Maybe Saxon had gotten himself a job, and married his lady. He decided to go ahead and ride in to find out.

***

The town was a good size, and looked to still be growing.

The main street was called Trail Street. He stopped in front of the sheriff's office, figuring that would be the best way to locate Andy.

He tied off the Tobiano and stepped onto the boardwalk. He opened the door and entered. A man wearing a badge looked up from his desk and sat back.

"Help ya?" he asked.

"Sheriff?"

"That's right," the middle-aged man said. "Sheriff Richards."

"I'm hoping you can help me find a friend of mine."

"Who might that be?" Richards asked.

"Andy Saxon."

"Saxon?"

Clint could see the man knew Andy.

"Why are you lookin' for a gunman like him?" Richards asked. "You lookin' to make a name for yourself?"

"No, nothing like that," Clint said. "I heard he was getting married. I was hoping to attend the wedding."

The sheriff stood up and grabbed his hat.

"Come with me."

"Where?"

"I'm gonna take you to Andy Saxon."

Clint followed the man out the door, and down the street. They reached the end of town and kept walking. Before long Clint knew where they were going.

They reached a collection of crosses and headstones. Richards led Clint to a grave that had no headstone, just a flat board with a name on it: Andy Saxon.

"When did he die?"

"About five weeks ago."

"How?"

"He was killed," Richards said. "Shot."

"Andy put up his guns."

"That's why he got killed," Richards said. "Shot down in the street."

"Before or after his wedding?"

"Before."

"And the woman?"

"Mary Ward," Richards said.

"Is she still living here?"

"Yes."

"I'd like to see her."

"I can take you to her," Richards said, "but I'd need to tell her who you are."

"My name's Clint Adams."

Richards looked at Clint with a shocked expression.

Chapter Four

"Why are we going to a saloon?" Clint asked, as they approached the Blue Bonnet Saloon.

"Mary Ward owns it," Sheriff Richards said.

"Did she own it when she met Andy Saxon?"

"She's owned it for a few years," Richards said. "What is the Gunsmith doin' here?"

"I told you," Clint said. "Saxon was my friend."

"But he's dead."

"I want to know who killed him, and why," Clint said.

"I don't know that," the lawman said.

"Are you going to find out?" Clint asked.

"I looked into it," Richards said, "but I didn't find anythin'. I ain't a detective."

"Then I'll find out," Clint said. "I'll talk to Mary Ward."

"Mr. Adams," Richards said, "I didn't want any trouble."

"I'm just going to talk with her."

"And after that, leave town," the lawman said.

"Let's see what I find out, Sheriff. Thanks for bringing me here."

"Let me know what you're gonna do."

The sheriff turned and walked away as Clint entered the saloon. It was early, and there weren't many customers. Clint went to the bar.

"Whataya have?" the bartender asked.

"Beer."

The bartender drew a beer and set it in front of him.

"Thanks."

"Two bits." the bartender said.

Clint set the two bits on the bar.

"Is Miss Ward in?" he asked, as the bartender scooped it up.

"She's in her office, upstairs."

"Can you tell her I'd like to see her?" Clint asked.

"I'll ask her," the barman said. "Wait here." He started away, then stopped and turned. "What's your name?"

"Clint Adams."

The bartender froze.

"For real?"

"That's my name."

The bartender thought a moment, then said, "Okay, wait here."

He went upstairs, and came back down in three minutes.

"Upstairs, first door at the top."

"Thanks."

Clint went up the stairs, leaving the beer on the bar. When he reached the door he knocked. It was opened by a lovely woman who glared at him.

"I should kill you," she snapped.

"I wouldn't blame you if you did."

She turned and walked away, leaving the door open. She was wearing a long-sleeved shirt, trousers and boots, with a bandana around her neck.

Clint entered the room and closed the door.

"Andy said you were his friend," she said.

"I was his friend," Clint said.

"You let him get killed."

"You talked him into putting his gun down," Clint said. "Did he stick to that?"

"He did."

"Then that's why he's dead."

She whirled on him.

"Why wouldn't you help him?"

"He wanted to hire my gun," Clint said. "I don't do that. He should have picked up his gun again and helped himself."

"What do you care?" she asked. "You kill people. That's what you do."

"That's not my reputation," Clint told her. "I use my gun to defend myself."

"Andy said you help people."

"I did help some people," Clint said, "but when I get involved in somebody else's business I end up killing people. I don't like it."

"So Andy's dead," she said. "You like that?"

"No, I don't like it," Clint said. "I think I made the wrong decision when I left. I thought he'd pick his gun up and help himself."

She slumped into a chair and stared at the floor.

"Then I got him killed," she said. "I know that."

"Miss Ward, I want to know who killed Andy."

"I don't know who killed him," she said. "He was shot down in the street. No one saw anything."

"Well," he said, "I'm going to stay in Bent Fork until I find out who did it. I feel I owe him that much."

"What does it matter?" she asked. "He's dead. You're just going to do it to make yourself feel better."

"You're probably right. Will you help me?"

"Why should I?" she demanded. She stood up and glared at him, again. "Get out! Just go away!"

"I'll be around for a while," he told her.

"I don't care."

She turned her back on him, and he left.

Chapter Five

Clint went back to the bar and picked up his beer.

"Want a cold one?" the bartender asked. "On the house."

"Sure."

The man took the half-filled mug and replaced it.

"What are you doin' here, Mr. Adams?"

"I was looking for Andy Saxon."

"Why?"

"We were friends," Clint said. "I want to know who killed him."

"I'd kinda like to know that, myself," the bartender said. "Andy was okay."

"What's your name?" Clint asked.

"They call me Max."

Clint studied the man for a moment. He was in his forties, with broad shoulders and arms lined with ropey muscles.

"Max, have you got any idea who might have killed him?" Clint asked.

"I wish I did."

"What about Maitland?" Clint asked.

"He bought Andy's ranch," Max said. "Why would he kill 'im?"

"The last time I saw Andy he said somebody was trying to force him to sell his ranch. Was that Maitland?"

"I dunno," Max said. "All I know is Andy suddenly decided to sell."

"Why did Mary want him to put his gun away for good?" Clint asked.

"She doesn't like guns," Max said. "She doesn't allow them worn in here."

Clint looked around, and noticed that the customers wore no guns.

"Where are they?"

"They turn them in when they come in. I keep 'em behind the bar. If you're gonna stay you'll have to turn yours in."

"That's not going to happen," Clint said. "If I walk around without a gun, I'll end up as dead as Andy. He should've kept his gun on."

"No argument from me," Max said.

"Tell me about the sheriff."

"What about him?"

"How hard did he look for Andy's killer?"

"I don't know that he looked at all," Max said.

"I need a hotel," Clint said.

"Down the street, the Webster House. It's decent."

"Thanks. Where's the livery?"

"End of Trail Street," Max said, "and if you want somethin' to eat, the Webster's got a good dining room."

"I'm going to be around, Max," Clint said, "if something occurs to you."

"Yeah, okay."

Clint left the saloon and walked his Tobiano to the livery. He arranged to have the horse cared for, then took his saddlebags and rifle and walked to the Webster Hotel.

"Room twenty-two the clerk said."

"Does it overlook a street?"

"No, sir, it's in the back."

"Good," Clint said. "Is the dining room open?"

"It's always open for guests, sir."

"I'll leave my things in my room and be back down in a few minutes."

"Very good, sir."

Clint went up, found a clean well-appointed room with a table, chairs, a bed, and dresser with a mirror over it. He dropped his things on the bed, washed up using the pitcher-and-basin in the dresser, and then went back down.

The dining room had about eight well-spread-apart tables, with only one occupied at the moment by a man seated alone. Clint chose a table on the other side of the room and ordered a bowl of beef stew.

The waiter brought the stew along with a basket of rolls and a mug of cold beer. The food was hot and satisfactory, although he felt there could have been more meat.

"Seems like more of a potato stew than beef stew, huh?" the man across the room said.

"I just wanted something in my stomach," Clint said. "This is fine."

The man got up and walked over, which Clint didn't like. He was wearing a three-piece suit and Clint figured he was some kind of drummer.

"My name's Herbert Luftin," the thirty-ish man said. He stuck his hand out, but Clint lifted his hands to show they were both full.

"I'm a drummer," the man confirmed, "selling ladies unmentionables."

Clint nodded.

"Doesn't seem like somethin' a man should be sellin', but I've also handled many other items."

Clint said, "I really don't like havin' a conversation while I'm eating, if you don't mind."

"Huh? Oh, of course, of course," the man said. "Please forgive the intrusion." He went back to his table and sat with his back to Clint, who finished his meal in peace.

Chapter Six

Clint finished his stew and washed it down with the beer. By that time the drummer had left the dining room, which suited him.

"Pie?" the waiter asked.

"What kind do you have?" Clint asked.

"Whatever you want," the man said. "There's nobody else here."

"Am I before or after the rush?" Clint asked.

"Before," the waiter said. "In about an hour some of the other guests will come down, and a few folks from outside."

"Peach?"

"Not the cook's specialty," the waiter said. "The apple is better."

"Apple then, and strong black coffee."

"Coming up."

The waiter brought the dessert out and set it down.

"Got a minute?" Clint asked.

"Sure," the waiter said, "longer." He sat.

"You know the people in town?"

"A lot of 'em."

"And Andy Saxton?"

"He's dead."

"I know," Clint said, "I'm trying to find out who killed him and why. You got anything?"

"Only that he coulda saved himself if he'd strapped his gun back on. He was fast."

"Doesn't matter how fast if he gave it up," Clint said.

"What's your interest?"

"He was a friend."

"And?"

"And I might've saved him, but I made a wrong decision."

"I don't know your name, but I can get it from the register."

"Clint Adams."

"Ah," the waiter said.

"What's your name?"

"Newly." The man was in his late thirties.

"How long have you worked here?"

"About five years."

"Worked here the whole time?"

"Yup."

The waiter sat back and stared at Clint. "So you're the Gunsmith."

"That's right."

"Was Andy ever as fast as you?" Newly asked.

"No."

"Who's the fastest you ever saw? Hickok? Earp? Masterson?"

"None of them."

"Really? Who?"

"Fella named Ben Thompson."

"I heard of him," Newly said. "Faster than you?"

"I wouldn't ever want to find out," Clint said. "Look, I'll pay for information."

"I don't want your money," Newly said. "Andy was a good man. Mary Ward got him all messed up."

"On purpose, you mean?"

"Naw, nothin' like that," Newly said. "After he sold his ranch he stayed here a few days. We got friendly. He was so in love with her he was willing to do anything. She made him put his gun down."

"I know that much," Clint said. "Do you think Maitland killed him? Or had him killed?"

"I'm gonna say maybe," Newly said. "Maitland has guns workin' for him."

"Tom Finn?"

"Naw, he's just a foreman," Newly said. "Some of the others. Among them a fella named Del Carrington. He's fast."

"Faster than Andy?" Clint asked.

"We'll never know," Newly said. "Andy was shot in the back."

Clint went stiff. He hated backshooters.

"I didn't know that," he said. "I just heard he was shot down in the street."

"He was bushwhacked."

"And he had already sold the ranch?"

"Yep."

"Why would Maitland have him killed if he already had the ranch?"

"That's a good question."

"What's your opinion of Sheriff Richards?"

"Pretty useless."

"That's what I was afraid of."

"He doesn't know it, though," Newly said. "He probably warned you out of town."

"He did."

Some people came into the room and Newly stood up.

"Gotta go to work," he said.

"Where can I see you later?"

"Saloon."

"The Blue Bonnet?" Clint asked.

"Naw," Newly said, "further down the street. The Lucky Lady."

"I'll see you there."

He paid his bill, gave Newly a big tip, and left.

Chapter Seven

It was almost dark when Clint stopped in the Lucky Lady Saloon. There was no sign of Newly, but the place was doing a decent business. He made a space for himself at the bar and ordered a beer.

"There ya go," the bartender said, setting it down. "You're a stranger here. What're you lookin' for?"

"Right now, I'm just after a cold beer," Clint said.

"You've got it."

"Thanks."

The bartender moved down the bar to serve other customers. At the moment, no one was paying attention to Clint.

Clint was halfway through the beer when Newly entered. By the time he reached the bar Clint had two more beers there, waiting.

"Thanks," Newly said, picking his up. "How far behind you am I?"

"Just one."

"Let's get a table," Newly said.

"One in the back," Clint said.

When they were seated Clint asked Newly, "You done for the night?"

"The dining room's closed til mornin'."

"Have you had any more thoughts about who killed Andy?" Clint asked.

"Why do you think I would?" Newly said. "I'm just a waiter."

"Waiters and bartenders," Clint said. "You both know a lot about what goes on in town."

"I do have one thought," Newly said, "about somebody else who knows what's goin' on."

"Who?"

"The town barber."

Clint hesitated, then said, "That's a good thought. How many barbers are in town?"

"Just one."

"Any others close by?"

"About seventy miles to the west."

"What's his name?" Clint asked.

"Lester," Newly said. "You're lookin' a little shaggy. You could use a haircut, and probably a shave."

"I think you're right," Clint said. "So far you've given me Carrington and Lester. Why?"

"I told you," Newly said. "I liked Andy."

"I did, too," Clint said, looking at his beer, "and I didn't help him much."

"You're feelin' guilty."

"I am."

"That mean you're gonna try to help Mary?" Newly asked.

"I already told her I wanted to find out who killed him," Clint replied.

"I mean help her to keep her saloon."

"Is she in danger of losing it?"

"Somebody's tryin' to force her out," Newly said, "like they tried to force Andy."

"I didn't know that," Clint said. "She just told me she wanted to kill me."

"She'll probably change her mind when she thinks about it," Newly said. "She's a smart lady."

"If she was smart she would've gotten Andy to help himself."

"He was committed to never picking up his gun, again," Newly explained.

"Then he was as much to blame for getting himself killed as I was."

"Oh, don't take so much guilt on yourself," Newly said. "He was more responsible."

"Maitland?"

Newly shrugged.

"Who knows?" he asked.

"I'm going to have to ask," Clint said. "Tell me, how much does Mary listen to her bartender, Max?"

"He's like a father to her," Newly said. "She'll listen to him."

"Okay," Clint said. "Maybe I can get to her through him."

"If you convince Max you can help, he'll convince her."

A saloon girl came over to the table, a pretty young blonde.

"Can I get you boys anythin'?" she asked.

"Two more beers, Lydia," Newly said.

"Comin' up."

"I don't need another one," Clint said, as she walked away.

"That's okay," Newly said. "I'll drink 'em both."

Clint stood up and put down enough money for the beers, plus some extra.

"Where you off to now? The Blue Bonnet?"

"Not tonight," Clint said. "I'm heading to my room for a good night's sleep. I rode a long time to get here. I'll get a fresh start in the morning."

"Then I'll see ya when you come down for breakfast," Newly said. "Steak and eggs?"

"Sounds good."

"It will be," Newly said. "I guarantee."

Chapter Eight

Clint had a good night's sleep and woke up refreshed and hungry. When he came down there were a few guests in the dining room, including the drummer.

" 'mornin', Mr. Adams," Newly greeted. "I kept a table for ya."

He followed Newly and sat down.

"Thanks," he said.

"Steak and eggs?" Newly asked.

"Definitely."

"Comin' up."

Clint sat back to await his breakfast and looked around. Only one person in the place was paying any attention to him, and it was the drummer. This time the man had his sample case with him, on the floor by his feet. Clint kept watching him until Newly returned with his breakfast.

"Newly, that fellow with the sample case."

"The drummer?"

"Yes," Clint said. "Do you know him?"

"Never saw him before."

"So he's not a regular?"

"Nope. Why?"

Clint shrugged.

"I don't like him."

Newly looked over at the man.

"Why not?" he asked.

"He just doesn't feel right. Do you know if he's checking out?"

"I have no idea," Newly said. "You think he's involved with Andy Saxon's death?"

"Was he here when Andy was killed?"

"No. He came some weeks later. In fact he came just before you did."

"Then he's not connected to what happened to Andy," Clint said. "But I still don't like him. He tried to get friendly while I was eating. I don't like talking to strangers, especially while I'm eating."

"Don't blame ya," Newly said. "I like eatin' alone, myself. You go ahead and eat and I'll keep folks away from you."

"Newly," Clint said, "does the town know I'm here?"

"Well, the sheriff knows, Mary and Max at the Blue Bonnet, and the folks here. I don't know if your name's gotten around more than that. I can tell ya one thing. I ain't told anybody."

"Thanks."

Newly went back to the kitchen as Clint started to eat. The steak was perfectly cooked, and the eggs were firm.

Clint was halfway through his steak-and-eggs when he noticed something. The drummer's suitcase was facing a different way. As he watched the man reached down into the case. Just as Clint dropped out of his chair there was a shot.

All the other diners dropped out of their chairs and hit the floor, looking around for where the shot had come from. Clint knew, though. The drummer was coming out of his case with a cut-off rifle, trying to bring it around to bear on Clint.

"Don't do it, Luftin, if that's your name."

The man froze.

"Drop the rifle."

As he dropped the gun, Clint walked towards him, and the other diners all ran from the room. Newly came out of the kitchen.

"Who is he?" the waiter asked.

"That's what I want to find out," Clint said. "Why don't you go and get the sheriff, Newly."

"Right!"

As Newly ran out Clint said, "Put that case on the table and open it."

"Luftin" did as he was told and opened the case. It was empty, which meant the only thing in it had been the cut-off rifle.

"What's this about?" Clint asked.

The man didn't answer.

"What's your real name?"

"It don't really matter," the man said, "Luftin'll do for now. At least, it'll do for the sheriff."

"Why'd you try to kill me?"

"I'd think you'd be used to this sort of thing happenin'," Luftin said. "After all, you *are* the Gunsmith."

"And how do you know that?"

The man smiled, seemingly at ease.

"You signed the register under your real name," he explained.

It was what Clint did most of the time, preferring not to hide under a phony name.

"Why don't we go out to the lobby to wait for the sheriff," Clint said. "Move!"

"Whatever you say, Mr. Adams," Luftin said. "You're hoidin' the gun."

Luftin moved out ahead of him and Clint paused only to pick up the rifle. Sheriff Richards may not have been a competent lawman, but he could certainly put the man calling himself "Luftin" into a cell.

Chapter Nine

"What's goin' on?" the sheriff asked, as he entered the lobby.

"I'm sure Newly told you something," Clint said.

"He said a drummer shot at you," Richards said. "This the fella?"

"This is him," Clint said. "He had this rifle in his case." He handed the lawman the weapon. "Says his name is Luftin."

"But that ain't his name, is it?"

"Probably not."

"Well, let's go."

"Where?" Luftin asked.

"To a cell, for a while," Richards said.

"Until when?"

"Until I find out who you are and why you're here in Bent Fork." He grabbed the man's arm. "Let's go."

"I'll walk over there with you," Clint said. "I want to know everything you find out."

"He's not gonna find out anythin'," Luftin said. He looked at Richards. "Trust me on that."

"Sheriff, you go ahead and take him in," Clint said. "I'll come by later."

"Whatever you say, Adams," Richards said. "Let's go."

The sheriff and "Luftin" left the hotel together. As they walked to the lawman's office the man said, "Sheriff, if I was you I'd talk to Mr. Maitland."

"Maitland?"

"Go and see him."

"Yeah, okay," Richards said. "After I put you in a cell, I'll go and see him."

"You better listen to him real good, Sheriff," "Luftin" said, "real good."

***

Clint went to the front desk to find out what room the drummer was in. When the clerk gave him the key to room 15 he went up.

"Come on up with me, Newly," he said to the waiter. "I just want a witness if I find anything."

"Sure, Mr. Adams."

They went up to room 15 and entered. Clint looked around while Newly stood by the door and watched.

"There's nothing here with his name on it," Clint said. "Just some extra clothes."

"Why do you think he tried to kill you?" Newly asked.

"I don't know," Clint said.

"Do you think it was because he recognized you?"

"It seems to me he must've planned it," Clint said. "Cut that rifle down to fit in the case. It wasn't a spur of the moment thing."

"You think the sheriff's gonna find out anythin'?"

"I don't know that either," Clint said. "I'll get over to his office and see. You better stay here and help your boss clean up."

"Yeah, okay," Newly said, "but let me know what happens."

"I will."

They left the room, and Clint left the hotel. When he got to the sheriff's office the lawman wasn't there, but Luftin was in a cell. There was also a young man sitting at the sheriff's desk.

"Where's the sheriff?" Clint asked.

"He had somethin' to do," the young man said.

"Are you a deputy?"

"Naw, I just keep an eye on the place when the sheriff's away. "I'm Barney."

"I want to talk to him."

"I know who you are, Mr. Adams," he said. "You go ahead and do whatever you want."

Clint approached the cell and asked Luftin, "What did you tell the sheriff?"

"I didn't tell him nothin'," the man said, "and I ain't gonna tell you nothin', either."

"We'll see about that," Clint said, approaching the cell.

Luftin smiled and said, "You ain't gonna shoot me while I'm unarmed and in this cell."

Clint turned and looked at the man seated at the desk.

"Hey, like I said," he spoke up, "you do anythin' you want."

Clint stared at the prisoner and said, "You're right. Maybe I'll just wait for you to get out. After all, you don't seem too worried about being in there."

"You're right, I ain't," Luftin said. "You ain't gonna be able to keep me in here."

"Well, then," Clint said, "I'll just wait for you to get out, before I put a bullet in you."

"Hey—"

"As soon as they let you out, I'll be outside waiting for you."

Luftin frowned.

"You can't just gun me down."

"Oh, you'll have your rifle in your hand."

"I don't have to," Luftin said. "I can come out unarmed."

"In that case," Clint said, "I'll just beat you to death."

"You wouldn't."

"Why not?" Clint asked. "You tried to bushwhack me while I was eating breakfast. And breakfast is my favorite meal."

Luftin stared at Clint and said, "You ain't that crazy."

"A coward like you doesn't deserve anything better," Clint told him.

"You better wait for the sheriff to come back," Luftin said. "He's gonna have somethin' to say about this."

"I don't care what the sheriff has to say," Clint said. "I make my own decisions."

"Whataya want from me?"

"I want to know your name, and who sent you after me."

Luftin sat back on his cot and crossed his arms.

"I think I'm just gonna wait for the sheriff to get back."

"Fine," Clint said. "Just know that I'll be waiting for you no matter when you get out."

"We gotta wait for the circuit judge," Luftin reminded him.

"I can wait," Clint said. "You tried to bushwhack me, I'll wait for you as long as I have to."

Clint walked out, leaving the worried man sitting on his cot. "Thanks," he said to the young man.

"Sure thing, Mr. Adams."

Clint decided to wait in the Lucky Lady Saloon for the sheriff to return.

He had a feeling he knew where the lawman had gone.

Chapter Ten

"A man tried to kill Adams and he didn't kill him?" Maitland asked.

"He wants to find out who sent him," Richards said.

"Do we know his name?"

"He says it's Luftin, but we don't believe him."

"What do you intend to do with him?" the older man asked.

"What can I do?" Richards asked. "I've got to hold him for the circuit judge. There were plenty of witnesses who saw him try to kill the Gunsmith. What else can I do?"

"You do just what you said you're gonna, Sheriff," Maitland said. "Do your job." He looked over at his foreman, Tom Finn. "Show the sheriff out."

"Yes, Sir."

As Richards left the office, Maitland crooked his finger at Finn.

"Get me Carrington."

"Yes, Sir."

Outside, Sheriff Richards asked Finn, "What's he got in mind?"

"Who knows?" Finn asked.

After the foreman watched the lawman ride off, he walked to the bunkhouse to fetch Del Carrington."

***

Finn walked into the office with Carrington.

"That's all, Finn," Maitland said.

"Yes, sir."

"Have a seat, Carrington."

The man sat, crossed a leg, and asked, "What's up?"

"I have a job for you."

"I hope you don't expect me to punch cows."

"That's not what I pay you for."

"Well, I was wondering when you'd let me do what you pay me for."

"There's a fella in the Bent Fork jail," Maitland said. "I don't want him getting out."

"He got a name?"

"He's calling himself Luftin."

"But that ain't his name, is it?" Carrington asked.

"No."

"Do I get to know his real name?" Carrington asked.

"No."

"How do I know I get the right guy?"

"There's nobody else in a cell, if you get it done to-night."

"Tonight it is, then."

"When you're done don't come straight back here," Maitland said.

"What about Clint Adams?"

"We'll deal with that later," Maitland said. "There's a line shack twenty miles west of here. There's enough food and water for you to wait there for me to call for you, again."

"I'm just supposed to sit and wait?"

"You can while away the time counting your money."

Carrington stood and accepted an envelope from Maitland.

"Suits me," he said.

"Then go," Maitland said. "You'll be hearing from me."

Carrington nodded and left. Maitland was sure he would hear from Sheriff Richards when the job was done.

He just hoped it would get done right.

***

Clint decided to wait in the Lucky Lady for the sheriff to return. He had a feeling he knew where the lawman had gone.

As he watched from the batwing doors of the Lucky Lady, Richards rode back to the office and tied his horse off before going in.

Chapter Eleven

Richards entered the office.

"Okay, Barney, thanks," he said. "You can go."

"Sure, Sheriff. Uh, you should probably know that Mr. Adams came here and talked to the prisoner."

"Did he find out anythin'?"

"I don't think so. They kinda yelled at each other."

"Okay, thanks, Barney."

"Sure, Sheriff."

Barney left and Richards went into the cell block.

"Hey, you're back," Luftin said. "Did you see Maitland?"

"I saw him," Richards said.

"So you're gonna let me out?"

"Not a chance," Richards said. "Not til the circuit judge gets here."

"What did Mr. Maitland tell you to do with me?"

"That's what he said," Richards answered. "Just wait."

"B-but he's the one who hired me," Luftin said. "He wants the Gunsmith dead."

"We'll see," Richards said. "You want somethin' to eat?"

"Yeah, sure, why not?"

"I'll be right back with a sandwich. Don't hurt your-self tryin' to get out of there."

Sheriff Richards left the office to walk to a nearby café.

***

Clint continued to watch, until Barney left, and then Richards. That meant Luftin was alone. He could go across, take him out of the cell, maybe take him to the livery and work on him. Maybe find out who hired him. But to do that he was sure he would have to beat him to within an inch of his life, and he didn't know if he was willing to do that. Maybe he should just wait for the circuit judge. He had enough witnesses to put "Luftin" away.

He turned and went back to the bar.

"Another beer?" the bartender asked.

"Naw, another saloon," Clint said. "Thanks."

"Only other place is the Bonnet," the man said, "and it ain't as good.'"

"I'll go and see," Clint said. "Maybe I'll be back."

As he started for the door he bumped into Newly.

"Mr. Adams!"

"Just call me Clint, Newly."

"Okay, Clint, where you headed?"

"The Blue Bonnet."

"Why? Beer's better here."

"Maybe," Clint said, "but I thought I could talk to Mary again."

"Better talk with Max, first," Newly said. "I'll come with you."

"Fine with me."

It was getting dark as they walked from the Lady to the Bonnet.

"Did you talk with the man who shot at you?" Newly asked.

"I did, but didn't find out anything," Clint said.

"What about the sheriff?"

"I don't know what he's doing," Clint said, "but right now he's keeping the man in a cell."

"And that satisfies you?"

"For now, it does."

When they got to the Bonnet they entered, found only a few customers at the bar and seated at a few tables.

"This place looks like it could be worth a lot of money," Clint said. "Why so few customers?"

"There's been trouble here," Newly said. "Nobody wants to get hurt."

They approached the bar.

"Hey, Max," Newly said.

"Newly."

"You know Mr. Adams?" Newly asked.

"I met 'im yesterday."

"Yeah, we met," Clint said. "How about two beers?"

"Comin' up," Max said.

He set two cold mugs in front of them.

"What brings you in tonight?" Max asked. "I heard somebody took a shot at you."

"Somebody did," Clint said. "He's in one of the sheriff's cells."

"Somebody hire him?" Max asked.

"He's not talking, but that's what I figure."

"And you think the sheriff's gonna find out who he is?" Max asked.

"I doubt it," Clint said, "but I'm willing to wait for the circuit judge."

"That could be days," Max said.

"I've got a hotel room," Clint said. "I'll wait."

"I figure if somebody tried to kill you, they'll try again."

"Max!"

They all turned to see who had called the bartender. At the top of the stairs Clint saw Mary Ward. She beckoned the bartender over, when he returned he said, "Mary wants to see you."

"First door top of the stairs, right?" Clint asked. "Thanks."

Chapter Twelve

Clint knocked on the door.

"Come in!" she called.

He opened it and stepped in. She was sitting in a chair with her legs crossed.

"I thought you only wanted to see me dead," he said.

"I heard somebody tried that, already," she said.

"Yeah, he did."

"Close the door and sit."

Clint did as was asked—or told.

"What's on your mind, Mary?" he asked.

"I think maybe I was too hard on you," she said. "You're right, Andy chose to keep his word to me and not pick up his gun. So I got him killed, not you."

"I think we can agree that whoever pulled the trigger killed Andy," Clint said. "And whoever was behind that is who I want."

"Do you think it's the same man who tried to kill you today?"

"Could be," Clint said. "A coward shot Andy in the back, and a coward tried to bushwhack me today."

"What are you going to do about it?"

"I told you, I'm not leaving town until I find the man who killed Andy."

"Then maybe you'll help me while you're here," she proposed.

"And you don't mind if I have to use my gun?" he asked.

"I already got one man killed," she said. "I'm not looking for another. If you agree to help me, I want you to do it your way."

"Okay, then," Clint said, "what do you want me to do?"

"Well, first I want you to find out who killed Andy . . ."

"And?"

". . . then I need help keeping my saloon."

"Who's after it?"

"The same man who bought Andy's place."

"Maitland!"

"He kept pushing Andy to sell, and when he finally did, he started pushing me."

"So where did Andy go after he left his ranch?"

"He came here to stay with me."

"So he was here when Maitland started pushing you."

"Yes. There was a fire, and someone tried to shoot me before they finally killed Andy."

"And you still wouldn't let him pick up his gun."

"I told him to do whatever he had to do, but he insisted on keepin' his word."

"He must've really been in love with you. When was the wedding supposed to be?"

She frowned and said, "I have to tell you something."

Clint waited, without prompting her.

"I never agreed to marry Andy," she said.

"What?"

"I told him I could never marry a man who lived by the gun," she said. "But I never said I'd marry him."

"So that was in his head?"

"I might've married him, but . . . up til the day he died, I never agreed."

"So you made a fool of him."

"No!" she snapped. "I was very fond of him, but . . . I never loved him like that. I guess he thought he could win me over."

"I guess we'll never know, now," Clint said.

Her eyes filled with tears as she hugged her upper arms.

"I'm sorry," she said. "I guess I am to blame for him bein' killed, not you."

"I feel my own degree of guilt, so I still owe him a deadly debt."

"Will you help me," she asked, "or should I just pack?"

"Let me look into Maitland some more," Clint said. "If I decide he had Andy killed, I'll do what I can to keep him off your back."

"Kill him?"

"If need be," Clint said, "but I doubt he's pulling the trigger himself. Do you know a man named Carrington?"

"No, who is he?"

"Apparently, a gunman hired by Maitland."

"And you don't know him?"

"Never heard of him," Clint said, "but I assume we're going to meet." He stood up. "Was there anything else?"

"No," she said. "The main thing I wanted to do was apologize."

"I appreciate that," he said, heading for the door.

She stood up and walked behind him. At the door she said, "You haven't said if you accept my apology."

"That's right," he said. "I haven't. Maybe another time."

"I suppose I deserve that."

"I'll stay in touch with Max. I understand he has a lot to say about what goes on here."

"Yes, he does. Max is the closest thing to a father I've ever had."

"We'll talk again," he said, and left.

Chapter Thirteen

Max set a cold one in front of Clint when he returned to the bar and asked, "What was that all about?"

"Apparently, you know," Clint said. "She wants my help hanging on to this place."

"Well, thank God for that," Max said. "Did you agree?"

"I did, although I wonder why. It sounds to me like she was stringing Andy along and made a fool of him."

"I know he was your friend," Max said, "but it seems to me Andy made a fool of himself. Mary never made any promises to him."

"That's what she said."

"Andy chose to believe she was going to marry him."

"Which is why he didn't pick his gun up."

"She told him not to put his gun down for her," Max said. "She made no promises."

"She said something about a fire."

"Yeah, in the back room. Lucky I was going back there to get something. I raised the alarm, and we got it out before it did much damage."

"And somebody took a shot at her?"

Max nodded and said, "On the street, before Andy was killed. I think it was just a warning."

"From who?"

"Good question."

"Maitland?"

"Maybe, but I won't point a finger at him just because he bought Andy's place."

"How much other property does he own?" Clint asked.

"A lot, including our competition, The Lucky Lady."

"Why's he want this place?"

"He wants the whole town."

"I'm tired of these people who want to own everything," Clint said. "That's just another reason for me to go against him."

"I really don't care why you do it, just as long as you do it."

Clint finished his beer and put the mug down.

"What happened to Newly?" he asked.

"He went back to the Lucky Lady."

"Is Maitland on that property very often?" Clint asked.

"He may own it, but he's never there," Max said. "He tends to stay on his ranch."

"I may have to go out there again," Clint said.

"Just be aware that Maitland has a number of guns workin' for him."

"I heard something about a man called Carrington."

"That's his top gun," Max said. "And he's fast. Keep an eye out for him."

"I intend to," Clint said. "Have you heard anything about him being a backshooter?"

"No," Max said. "Every gunfight I've heard of him bein' involved in has been face-to-face."

"I'll keep that in mind. Keep an eye on Mary."

"I always do," Max said.

Clint moved to go out the batwing doors when he heard a shot from across the street. He ran out and stopped, waiting for a second shot, but it didn't come.

Max came out behind him, holding a shotgun.

"Where'd it come from?" he asked.

"I don't know, but I'm going to check the jail."

"Want me to back you up?" Max asked.

"No, just stay here and keep an eye on Mary."

"Right."

Clint ran across the street toward the jail, almost expecting the front door to open, but it didn't. When he got there, he opened the door and ran in. Sheriff Richards was coming out of the cell block, looking harried.

"Sheriff?" Clint said.

"He's dead," the lawman said, "Somebody shot Luftin through the window."

"Check outside," Clint said.

Richards ran out the door, while Clint sprinted into the cell block, grabbing the keys from the wall. Luftin was sprawled on the floor. Clint unlocked the cell door and crouched over him. He was definitely dead, shot once.

Clint went to the window and looked out. It was off an alley, easily accessible. Then he saw Sheriff Richards.

"Anything?" Clint called.

"No sign of anyone."

"Come back inside, then."

"Right."

Clint went into the office and waited. When the door opened and Richards came in he told the Sheriff, "Drop your gun."

"What?"

"You heard me. Drop it."

Richards stared at him and asked, "What's this about?"

"You're tense," Clint said. "Don't even think about drawing. You'll never make it."

Clint saw all the tension go out of Richards' body.

"That's good. Now drop the gun."

Richards took his gun from the holster and dropped it to the floor.

"I only have your word that somebody else shot Luftin, not you," Clint said. "Convince me."

Chapter Fourteen

"What do you say happened?"

"I don't know," Richards said. "I was sitting at my desk and heard a shot. I ran into the cell block and saw Luftin on the floor. When I ran out you were here. That's it, that's all."

"And you don't know who shot him, huh?"

"No idea."

"And you didn't do it."

"Why would I?"

"That's a good question."

"Adams, I don't have the guts to shoot a man in a cell."

"It doesn't seem that would take much guts," Clint said. "Maybe just some money."

Richards bristled.

"I may not be your idea of a good lawman," he said, "but I wouldn't shoot a man in cold blood."

"So you say," Clint said. "Where did you go this afternoon?"

Richards hesitated, then said, "I went to see Mr. Maitland."

"Why?"

"Luftin told me to," Richards said. "I thought Maitland might tell me something useful."

"And did he?"

"No. In fact he didn't tell me nothin', I told him I had Luftin in a cell."

"And what did he say?"

"That I should just do my job and keep him there."

"Until when?"

"Til the circuit judge arrived."

Clint paused to think a moment.

"Do you think Maitland sent somebody to kill Luftin?" the lawman asked.

"Could be."

"But why?"

"So he couldn't tell anybody that Maitland hired him."

"So you think Maitland hired Luftin to kill you, and then sent someone to kill him?"

"It's very possible."

"And you're thinkin' Maitland had Andy Saxon killed?"

"Could be," Clint said. "Once you start something like that, it gets easier."

"Who's he usin' for all that?"

"You know about Carrington, right?" Clint asked.

"I know Carrington ain't a bushwhacker," Richards said. "He likes doin' his killin' face-to-face."

"That would suit me," Clint said. "There's nothing I hate more than backshooters and bushwhackers."

"Well, Adams," Richards said, "Ya gotta believe me. I didn't kill this fella callin' himself Luftin." I ain't got no reason to."

Clint stared at the man, then said, "You better get the undertaker over here."

The lawman breathed a sigh of relief when he realized Clint wasn't going to kill him. He started out the door, then stopped and turned back.

"Can I pick up my gun?"

"Go ahead."

Richards kept his eyes on Clint as he bent to pick it up, and then walked out.

For want of something better to do, with only a dead body for company, Clint sat at the sheriff's desk to consider the matter. It was obvious somebody hired "Luftin" to kill him. Obviously, he was only given one chance. He wondered who was killed after the first failed attempt on Mary Ward's life.

And who would be sent after him now? Del Carrington?

He decided the thing to do was to go and see Frank Maitland, at least to find out if he knew a man named Luftin.

When the door opened, Sheriff Richards entered, followed by a small man in a dark suit.

"This is the undertaker, Ed Cryer," Richards said.

"I've got some men comin' to collect the body," Cryer said.

"That's fine," Clint said.

Cryer started for the cell block, then stopped and turned.

"I also sent for the doctor."

"I guess you all have a job to do," Clint said. "I'll just get out of the way."

"What do you intend to do now?" Richards said.

"Just what I've been doing," Clint said, "I'm going to talk to people."

"Maitland?"

"Don't worry about it," Clint said, "You just get that body out of your jail."

"But—"

Clint didn't wait, he just turned and left. He came face-to-face with a tall, elderly man outside.

"Doctor?"

"That's right."

"Mr. Cryer's inside," Clint said.

"But who are yo—"

Clint didn't wait. He turned and walked away. He was going to make his first stop at the Blue Bonnet, to talk with Mary Ward and Max, again.

Chapter Fifteen

Clint stopped at the bar first.

"Max, is Mary in her room?"

"She is. I guess you can go up."

"In a minute. Max, have you met Frank Maitland?"

"If you mean have I been introduced to him, no. I'm a bartender. I've seen him and spoken to him to ask him what he wants to drink, but no, I haven't actually been introduced to him."

"So you don't know anything about him?"

"No, you'd have to talk to Mary. She spent some time with him when he was trying to buy the place."

"And if I needed to talk to somebody about him, somebody who knows him. who would that be?"

"Well, he owns the Lucky Lady," Max said. "Talk to somebody over there."

"Who runs it for him?"

"Fella named Sam Giles."

"Are they friends?"

"Naw, Giles just works for him."

But first I'll talk to Mary."

"Go on up."

"Thanks."

Clint went up and knocked on Mary's door.

"Come in," she said, when she opened it. "What happened?"

"Somebody shot the man in his cell," Clint said. "Does this sound like something Frank Maitland would do?"

"I wouldn't put anything past him," she said. "He was very angry when I turned down his first offer. He said I'd wish I had accepted."

"When he came to see you, was he alone?"

"Frank Maitland never goes anywhere alone."

"He spoke with me alone, but we were on his ranch. There were men all around."

"He must've felt safe," she said.

"Well," Clint said, "if he still feels safe, maybe he'll tell me something."

"You're going to see him again?"

"Yes."

"But if he tried to kill you, what's to stop him from trying again?"

"I don't think he'd do it in his own home."

"You mean Andy's home," Mary said. "I still think of it as his."

"Maybe I'll take that tactic and see how Maitland acts," Clint said.

"You mean make him mad and see what he does?" she asked.

Clint nodded.

"Maybe you should take somebody with you," she suggested.

"I don't have anybody and there's no time for me to find someone.

Well, let me know what happens," she said. "And try not to get killed."

"I'll do my best."

Clint left the room and went back down. He stopped at the bar on the way out.

"She help you?" Max asked.

"She tried."

"What are you gonna do now?" Max asked.

"I'm riding out to Maitland's ranch for a talk," Clint said. "I want to see what kind of reaction I can get from him."

"You're goin' out there alone?" Max said. "You want some company? Me and my shotgun?"

"That's okay, Max," Clint said. "I think I can handle it."

"If I was you, I'd watch out for Del Carrington."

"Have you seen him, lately?" Clint asked.

"Not in here," Max said. "Not even in town. But he might be out there."

"I guess I'll find out," Clint said, and walked out.

***

Clint went to the livery and saddled his Tobiano. He walked the horse outside and mounted up. As he rode down Trail Street Sheriff Richards came out of his office and waved.

"Are you sure you wanna do this, Adams?" he asked. "Ride out to see Mr. Maitland?"

"I'm just going to push a bit and see what happens," Clint said.

"I don't know Maitland all that well, Mr. Adams," Richards said, "but I think I can say he doesn't push easily."

"I guess I'll have to find that out for myself," Clint said. "Is the body at the undertakers?"

"It is."

"And what did the doctor have to say?"

"One shot to the back of the head."

"One bushwhacker killing another," Clint said. "Perfect."

"What makes you think you won't be bushwhacked, yourself?" Richards asked.

"I can't say for sure I won't," Clint said, "but I'll do my best to avoid it."

"I hope you do, avoid it," Richards said. "I really hope you do."

Chapter Sixteen

When the foreman, Tom Finn, saw Clint ride up to the house he walked over. Some hands watched from the corral and barn.

"Mr. Adams, what brings you back?"

"I'd like to talk to Mr. Maitland, again," Clint replied.

"I can take you to him," Finn said, "but will I need to bring a gun?"

"What for?"

"Maybe you can tell me."

Clint laughed.

"I don't anticipate any gunplay, Mr. Finn," Clint said. "That is, unless Del Carrington's around."

"Are you lookin' to try Carrington?" Finn asked. "He's the fastest I've ever seen."

"I'm not interested in Carrington, at all," Clint said. "I just want to talk to Mr. Maitland. No guns."

"All right," Finn said. "Wait here, please."

"Thanks."

Clint watched Finn walk into the house . . .

***

Finn entered the house, and walked down the hall to Frank Maitland's office.

"What are you doing here?" Maitland asked, looking up from his desk.

"Clint Adams is outside," Finn said. "He wants to see you."

"Does he have a gun?"

"He always has a gun," Finn said, "but he says he's not interested in gunplay."

"What else would he say?" Maitland opened a desk drawer, took out a gun, checked, and returned it.

"All right," he said, "bring him back."

"And stay?"

"Sure," Maitland said, "he might not try anything with a witness."

"You got any idea what this is about, boss?"

"I do," Maitland said, "but it's none of your affair, Tom."

"He asked me about Carrington, boss."

"What did you tell him?"

"Nothin'," Finn said. "I just said that Carrington was the fastest I'd ever seen."

"Okay," Maitland said, "bring the Gunsmith in."

"Yes, Sir."

***

When Finn came back out he beckoned to Clint.

"Mr. Maitland will see you in his office. Follow me."

Clint followed the foreman into the house and to the office. As he entered, he saw Maitland sitting behind his desk.

"To what do I owe this visit?" the man asked.

"I've been hearing things about you, Mr. Maitland," Clint said.

"What kind of things?"

"I've been told you have gunmen working for you. Gunmen like a man named Carrington."

"That's ridiculous," Maitland said. "I have a hand named Carrington working for me, but he's no gunman."

"Where is he?" Clint asked.

"He's out with some of the hands," Maitland said. "Should be back in a couple of days."

"Do you know a man named Luftin?"

"No, I don't think so. Who is he?"

"A hired gun paid to kill me. He didn't get the job done, and somebody had him killed for missing."

"That's terrible," Maitland said. "Wait a minute. You think I'm trying to have you killed?"

"I think whoever had Andy Saxon killed is trying to have me killed, too. Apparently he also tried to have Mary Ward killed."

"What? Why try to have her killed?"

"It could be because she won't sell her place."

"And you heard that I made an offer on her place."

"That's right, I did."

"I'm a businessman, Mr. Adams," Maitland said. "I don't employ gunmen, or have people killed when they won't sell to me."

"Well, you seem to be the only one in town who could afford these things."

"Preposterous!" Maitland shouted. "There are other businessmen and ranchers in the area."

"I see. And do you think they're the kind of men I'm looking for?"

"No, I don't," Maitland said. "But I don't think I am, either."

Clint looked at Finn.

"Can you think of anyone?"

"Me? Hell, I can't think of anyone. And I sure wouldn't say my boss is that kind of man."

"Thanks for the vote of confidence, Finn," Maitland said. "Is that all, Mr. Adams?"

"I guess so."

"Good. Finn will show you the way out."

"Thanks for your time, Mr. Maitland."

Clint followed Finn through the house and out the front door. They stopped at his horse.

"What about it, Finn?" Clint asked. "Anything you want to tell me now that we're not in front of your boss?"

"What? Oh, no," Finn said. "I don't know nothin' else. I think you're barkin' up the wrong tree."

"What do you know about Del Carrington?"

"Just that he works for us?"

"And have you ever heard of a man called Luftin? Supposed to be a drummer."

"Not a thing. What's he sell?"

"Well, the only thing he had in his case was a sawed-off rifle."

"Where was he killed?"

"In his jail cell."

"Somebody shot 'im in cold blood in a cell?"

"That's right."

"So Saxon was bushwhacked, somebody tried to bushwhack you, and then he was killed?"

"That's right."

"And you said somebody tried to kill Miss Ward?"

"Took a shot at her in the street."

Finn shook his head.

"What the hell is goin' on?" the foreman asked.

"That's exactly what I'm trying to find out, Mr. Finn," Clint said, before mounting up and riding away.

Chapter Seventeen

Before riding away, Clint called out to Finn, "Do you have any idea where Carrington is now?"

"The only place I think he could be is a line shack in the east forty," Finn said. "We've got some strays out there."

"Thanks."

Finn watched as Clint rode away, then went back into the house. Maitland looked up as he reentered the room.

"Did you tell him?" the rancher asked.

"Yeah," Finn said, "the line shack. But why—"

"Never mind," Maitland said. "Just get somebody out there to warn him."

"What do you think will happen when Adams finds him?" Finn asked.

"When two men like that meet head-to-head?" Maitland said. "What do you think?"

"But—"

"Go ahead, get it done. And then get back to work."

"Yes, sir."

Finn left. Maitland sat back and wondered what, indeed, would happen when two men like that met?

***

Halfway back to Bent Fork, Clint had a chance to make up his mind to continue on or ride out to find that line shack. If he could talk to Carrington alone without Maitland around, maybe he'd find out something. That was if he convinced Carrington not to draw before they could talk.

He turned his horse and rode away from town.

***

He found the line shack late in the day. There was one horse tied off outside, a rangy colt. Clint reined in his Tobiano some distance away and tied it to a tree, then approached the shack. Before he reached the shack the door opened and a tall man stepped out. He was as rangy as his horse. He wore a gun in a holster on his left side.

"Adams?" he said.

"Good guess."

"How'd you find me out here?"

"Guess."

"Maitland?"

"Actually, it was Finn," Clint said, "but Maitland probably told him to send me here."

"You think he figured one of us would kill the other?" Carrington asked.

"I don't even think it matters who kills who."

"Why would he want me dead?"

"I'm thinking he's done with you," Clint said. "You've already killed for him."

Carrington laughed.

"Who have I killed?"

"Saxon? Liftin?"

"I didn't kill Andy Saxon. I never would've killed him while he wasn't wearing a gun."

"And Luftin? He was sitting in a cell."

"Again, I don't kill unarmed men. I kill head-to-head," he waved. "Like this."

"But not for no reason?"

"There's usually a reason."

"Like seeing who's fastest?" Clint asked.

"That could be a reason."

"And what if Maitland's paying?" Clint said. "You want to test me for his money?"

"I'd rather just find out for myself," Carrington said. "Wouldn't you?"

"No," Clint said.

"Why not? Scared?"

"I just don't care which one of us is faster," Clint said. "It's not important to me."

"It's important to all of us. You think Hickok didn't care? Earp? Clay Allison?"

"Okay, some of them cared, like Allison. But Bill was my friend, and Earp is my friend. They don't care."

"You know what?" Carrington said. "Come on in. We'll have a drink."

Carrington turned his back on Clint and went inside. If he trusted Clint enough to do that, he decided to follow him, closing the door behind them.

Chapter Eighteen

Inside was a simple, handmade table, chairs, and a cot.

"Have a seat," Carrington said. "I've got some whiskey and a couple of glasses."

Clint sat and Carrington brought the glasses and bottle to the table. He poured a few inches into each glass and pushed one toward Clint.

"What are you doing out here?" Clint asked.

"Maitland sent me here to wait."

"For what?"

Carrington shrugged.

"For whatever and wherever he needs me."

"So if he sends you after me . . ."

"He better have a good reason."

"What about Andy Saxon?" Clint asked. "If you didn't kill him, who did?"

"I don't know," Carrington said. "Some coward who did it for money."

"Paid by who?" Clint asked. "Maitland?"

"It wouldn't surprise me."

Clint downed his whiskey and stood up.

"Are you going to stay here and wait?" he asked.

"As long as I work for Maitland, yes," Carrington said.

"And how did you know I was coming?"

"Maitland sent a man to warn me."

"He's going to be disappointed when he realizes we're both alive," Clint said.

Carrington stood up and walked outside with Clint.

"Adams," he said, "we're probably gonna face off at some point."

"Well, if it happens," Clint said, "I hope it'll be because you want to, and not because you're being paid to."

"I guess we'll see."

Clint walked to his Tobiano and mounted up. He wasn't sure if Carrington was telling the truth or not. He did believe him about not killing Andy Saxon. If Saxon had been wearing his gun, Carrington would've faced him. When the time came, Carrington would face Clint in the street. He just hoped they would be facing each other for a reason, and not just to find out who's faster.

That was always a waste of time.

***

Clint rode back to Bent Fork, assuming the man known as Luftin was in a grave. He left his Tobiano in the livery and went to the sheriff's office.

"I wondered when you'd be back," Richards said, from behind his desk. "Where's you been?"

"I saw Maitland, talked to the foreman, Finn, and then rode out to a line shack to see Carrington."

"You faced Carrington?"

"I had a drink with him."

"No gunplay?"

"Not this time," Clint said. "You get the drummer buried?"

"The undertaker took care of it."

"Good."

Clint turned and started for the door.

"Hey!" Richards asked, "what did you accomplish?"

Clint just said, "Not much," and left.

He was going to go to the Blue Bonnet and see Mary. It wouldn't do any good to tell the sheriff about his conversations. After all he still didn't trust the lawman. In fact, he didn't have anyone in town to trust, not even Max and Mary. They could have their own intentions.

He entered the Bonnet and approached the bar, where there was plenty of space.

"Mary's upstairs," Max said, putting a beer down. "Did you see Maitland?"

"I did."

"Find out anythin'?" the bartender asked.

"Nothing he didn't want me to know."

"So you still don't know who pulled the trigger on Andy," Max said.

"No, but I'm closer to finding out."

"And how's that going to happen?"

"I think we'll just have to wait and see." He picked up his beer. "I'm going up and see Mary."

"Listen to what she says," Max said. "She has her own idea about what's goin' on."

"I'm sure she does," Clint said. "Don't worry, I'll listen to the girl."

Clint walked to the stairs and up to Mary's door, where he knocked. When she answered and saw him, she reached out and grabbed his arm, tugging him into the room.

"You must know something, by now," she said. She pulled him to the bed and they sat. "Tell me what you've got."

"I've got nobody admitting anything," Clint said,

"But did you talk to Maitland?"

"I did, as well as his foreman, and top gun."

"You faced his top gun and didn't kill 'im? Why not?"

"I didn't have to."

Chapter Nineteen

"What do you mean, you didn't have to?"

"Mary, I don't kill unless I have to."

"I don't understand," she said. "You live by your gun. Like Andy did."

"He did until he put his gun down," Clint said. "Then he died by his gun. No, by somebody else's gun."

"And isn't Mr. Maitland going to send gunmen after you?" she asked.

"He might, but apparently he's not ready for that," Clint said. "He's probably still going to make you an offer for this place."

"And when I say no? He'll try to kill me?"

"If he does he has to go through me," Clint said.

"It sounds like he had a chance to kill you, today," she said.

"Well, for one, he wasn't prepared to do it himself and, for two, his top gun wasn't ready."

"You faced him? What was his name? Carrington?"

"That's right, Del Carrington."

"You're not gonna have to face him?" she asked.

"I probably will," Clint said, "but when he's ready."

"You're gonna let him—how do you say it —call the play?"

"Why not?" Clint asked. "I'm hoping he'll call it, and not Maitland."

"When will you go after Maitland for killing Andy?"

"When I'm sure he was responsible, and when I know who pulled the trigger."

"What if I told you I wanted you to do it now?" she asked. "Do it for me."

"Mary, you have the wrong idea about why I'm here," he said. "I came here for Andy. I'm going to find who killed him. In the meantime, I'll do what I can for you."

She slapped him across the face and said, "You're a sonofabitch! I want you to help me! Do it for me! I told you I didn't love Andy."

"Andy was my friend. I'm not concerned about whether or not you loved him."

He got up and walked to the door, but before he could open it she was on his back, pulling him to the bed.

"You sonofabitch!" she growled again when she had him on his back and climbed atop him, kissing him fiercely. She was a good-sized woman, solid and heavy, and kept him pinned down. Instead of trying to fight her off, he wrapped her arms around her and held her tightly, kissing her back. Eventually, she stopped fighting to keep him down and they concentrated on kissing each other. He slid out from beneath her and while she slipped out of her clothes, he removed his gun, hung it on the bedpost, and then undressed. When they were both naked, they came together again on the bed in a hot, feverish embrace.

She worked her way atop him again and slid down on his long, hot pole, taking it inside her. Grabbing hold of the bedpost, she began to ride him up and down. Slowly he matched her rhythm and then they began to move together. Abruptly, her hand encountered his gun and it made her mad.

"Does this have to be here?" she demanded, grabbing, to toss it away.

He took her by the wrists and stopped her.

"The gun has to be there!" he snapped. "If you want to keep doing this, it has to stay there!"

She glared at him, and then said, "Fine, just fine! If you need a gun to fuck me, so be it!"

She abandoned any attempts to grab the gun, and went back to what they were doing, slamming into each other as he drove in and out of her, so violently they grunted with each thrust . . .

***

When they finished, instead of rolling into his embrace, she rolled away from him, facing the other way.

He stared at her back for a while before talking.

"You're going to have to get over this thing about guns," he said.

"I know," she said, meekly. "If you put your gun down you'll end up dead."

"That's right."

"Like Andy."

"Exactly."

She pulled the sheet up to her neck and turned to face him.

"All right," she said. "What can I do to help you?"

"Just stay in the saloon with Max, so I don't have to worry about you."

"Why don't you take Max to help you?" she suggested.

"I'd have to worry about him, too," Clint said, getting out of bed.

"You're goin'?" she asked.

"I better," Clint said. "As long as I'm around you, there's a chance you can be hurt."

After he dressed and strapped on his gun he went to the door.

"Watch your back, Clint." she said.

"That's what I intend to do."

He walked out.

Chapter Twenty

Clint went back to the bar for another beer with Max.

"Let me see that shotgun," Clint said.

Max took it out from behind the bar and put it on top. It was a double-barrel, over-and-under weapon. From behind the bar a shot would take out half-a-dozen men.

"Keep it close at all times," Clint said. "I still don't know what Saxon's killer is after."

"And the man in the cell," Max said.

"Yes, if they were killed by the same man."

"What about Mary?" Max asked.

"Keep her inside, where she's safe, and keep her away from windows."

"Got it. What about the sheriff? He backin' you?"

"I'm not sure yet where he stands, but I think I'll keep him in sight."

"That means stayin' in his office?"

"Right. That's where I'll be."

He finished his beer and left the Bonnet.

"Hey, Clint!"

He turned to see who was calling him and saw Newly, the waiter, running across the street to him.

"Newly!" He grabbed the boy's arm and pulled him onto the boardwalk. "Stay off the street."

"Is there gonna be shootin'?"

"There's no telling what's going to happen," Clint said. "I want you to stay inside."

"Are you comin' back to the hotel?" Newly asked. "You need a meal?"

"I'm going to stay in the jail with the sheriff for a while," Clint said. "I'll eat whatever he gets brought in."

"Ugh! He eats in the Forty-Four Caliber Café. Their food tastes like they make it with gunpowder."

"Never mind," Clint said. "Just stay inside till it's all over."

"Yeah, okay."

"Go ahead."

He watched the young man run back to the hotel, then turned and continued on to the sheriff's office.

***

As Clint walked in Richards said, "I was about to make my rounds."

"I'll go with you," Clint said.

"You gonna be my new deputy?"

"Not a chance. I'm just sticking close because I don't trust you."

"Well, that might keep me alive, too, so I'll take it."

They left the office to walk the streets together, checking if the door was, indeed, locked.

"What about the saloons?" Clint asked when they were heading back to the office.

"They close at three," Richards said. "We'll do rounds again, then."

"What about something to eat?" Clint asked.

"I'll get something from the Forty-Four Caliber in a while."

"We'll go together," Clint said.

"I'll eat later," Richards said, as they reached the door. When he opened it, and they stepped in Clint smelled the food immediately.

"I brought somethin' over," Newly said. "At least you'll eat well."

"Get back to the hotel!" Clint snapped.

"I'm goin', I'm goin'."

"And stay there," Clint added. "Don't bother picking up the plates."

"Yes, sure."

Clint saw Newly to the door and locked it. When he turned around, Richards was looking at the food Newly had set out on the desk.

"This is sure gonna be better than the Forty-Four Caliber's food," Richards said. "Pull that chair over."

Clint pulled a chair over and sat across from Richards. Newly had supplied knives, forks and mugs of beer. They picked up their utensils and started to cut into their steaks.

"This is perfect," Richards said. "I'm used to hackin' away at well-done steaks. These are red and done perfect."

I think maybe I'll offer you the deputy's job," Richards said, "that is, once you trust me."

"Not interested," Clint said. "I'm just interested in eating, right now, and staying alive."

"I gotta agree with you, there."

Clint looked around, then said, "I'm gonna pull these curtains, and we'll stay away from the windows."

"That suits me," Richards said.

Clint got up, pulled the curtains, and returned to his meal. They poured coffee from the office pot and ate the apple pie Newly had brought over.

When they were done Clint moved the trays over to a small table against the wall, with wanted posters on the wall above.

"I got some cards," Richards said. "Two-handed poker?"

"Why not?"

Chapter Twenty-One

Richards and Clint went on rounds again. Afterward, each took a cell to sleep in. The lawman slept soundly while Clint slept lightly, listening to the man snore.

As the sun came up, and the sheriff kept snoring, Clint stood and stretched, strapped on his gun and walked out into the office. He went to the window, pulled aside the curtain and gazed out. There was nobody on the street yet, as the sun was rising.

He turned and walked to the desk, sat behind it and, for want of something better to do, started going through drawers.

In a bottom one, he came across a bunch of posters like the ones on the wall. He took them out and started leafing through them.

"The up-to-date ones are on that wall," Sheriff Richards said, exiting the cell block.

"I wasn't sure if you kept track," Clint said.

He walked to his desk and Clint vacated it.

"Sometimes it's all I have to do," Richards said. "Are we gettin' breakfast from the hotel?"

"I told him no, but who knows?" Clint asked. "Let's give it some time before we go to the Forty-Four Caliber."

"After eatin' that hotel food I don't know if I can go back to that café."

As it turned out, Newly appeared at eight a.m. with a tray, and traded it for the supper tray from the night before. He brought ham-and-eggs, biscuits, and orange juice. He remembered that the jail had its own coffee pot.

"I'll be back tonight with supper," Newly said, and Clint decided not to try to talk the young man out of it.

They ate their breakfast and washed it down with coffee from the office pot, which was strong enough for Clint.

"Adams, what do you think are the chances Maitland will send some men after you?" Richards asked after a while.

"The talk I had with Carrington makes me believe that Maitland can't just point him at me. Carrington might be just a little bit too much his own man for that."

"I hope you're right," Richards said. "But even if you are, he's got other guns."

"We'll just have to wait and see what happens," Clint said.

"It's got to depend on how bad he wants to own Bent Fork. If he gets rid of me, he can take over the town place-by-place."

"Startin' with the Bonnet?"

"Well, he owns several businesses already," Clint said, "and he's made offers for the Blue Bonnet. If he was smart he'd bypass the Bonnet and move on, then come back to it. But I don't think his ego will let him do that."

"Then he'll probably make a move against you, eventually."

"Or," Clint said, "I could convince him that I'm leaving, and see if he comes out of hiding."

***

Del Carrington rode up to Maitland's house, and Finn came over to intercept him.

"Did the boss send for you?" Finn asked, as Carrington dismounted.

"No, he thinks I'm still in the line shack. But Adams found me there."

"And you killed him?" Finn asked.

"No," Carrington said, "we talked?"

"Talked? That's all?"

"It was enough," Carrington said. "Now I wanna talk to Maitland. Take me to him."

"Wait here and I'll—"

"Let's just go in," Carrington said, and started up the stairs. Finn ran after him.

As they went down the hall to Maitland's office, Finn hurried ahead of Carrington and said, "At least let me tell him you're coming."

"Yeah, go ahead," Carrington said.

Finn entered the office and started to say, "Carrington's here—" but the gunman came in right behind him.

"What are you doing here?" Maitland demanded.

"I wanted you to know that Adams found me at the line shack, and we're both still alive."

"What are you talking about?"

"You wanted one of us dead," Carrington said. "Neither of us is."

"And why is that?" Maitland asked, sitting back in his chair.

"Clint Adams has a code of ethics," Carrington said. "I convinced him I do, too."

"So what does that get me?" Maitland asked.

"He's convinced that if I kill him, it won't be for you, it'll be for me."

"So why didn't you just shoot him when his back was turned?" Maitland asked.

"Because I wouldn't shoot a man like Clint Adams in the back," Carrington said. "He deserves better than that.

Besides, I didn't want to kill him out there in the middle of nowhere. No one would see."

"So, you're saying you do have a code of ethics?" Maitland asked.

"I'm saying when I kill Adams it'll be face-to-face, in the street, where everybody can see it happen."

Maitland laughed.

"So much for your code of ethics."

"Well, I'm not gonna hide in a line shack any longer," Carrington said. "If you want me to take care of the Gunsmith, I need to know a little—no, a lot more, about what's going on."

"Is that a fact?"

Carrington sat down and said, "Unless you have another top gun to send after him? Like Finn?"

"No," Maitland said, "no other top guns." He looked at his foreman. "Certainly not Finn. He's got his own job to do. And he better get to it."

"Yes, sir."

The foreman left the office and Maitland studied Carrington.

"All right," he said, finally, "maybe you're right. If I want you to face a man like the Gunsmith, I suppose you should be brought up to date."

"Good," Carrington said, "why don't we start with you telling me who killed Andy Saxon?"

Chapter Twenty-Two

"What do you mean?" Sheriff Richards asked. "You're gonna leave town?"

"I'm wondering if I did leave town, what Maitland's next move would be?"

"I don't get it," Richards said. "Are you leavin' or not?"

"I'm going to make it look like I am," Clint said. "Then I'll keep my eye on Maitland and see what happens."

"I can watch for him here in town."

"No," Clint said, "I don't want you anywhere near him, Sheriff."

"Whataya mean?"

"If Maitland happens to discover that I didn't leave town, I don't want to have any reason to suspect that you told him."

"So I'm supposed to avoid him?"

"At all costs," Clint said. "And since I'll be watching him, that means I'll see if you talk to him."

"You really don't trust me, do you, Adams?" Richards asked.

"Not at all, but don't take it personal," Clint said. "I don't trust anyone."

"So you suspect me of killin' Andy Saxon and that fake drummer?"

"I told you, I suspect everyone."

"You think I shot Saxon, and that man in my own jail cell?"

"I don't know what you did, Sheriff, or if you did anything," Clint said. "But I'm going to find out."

"So you want me to stay here in my office until you're finished?"

"Just stay away from Maitland, Sheriff," Clint said. "I don't care who else you talk to."

"When do you intend to leave—or make it look like you left?"

"I'm going to check out of the hotel tomorrow morning and ride out."

"How do you expect Maitland to know that you've left town?" Richards asked.

"I assume he's got somebody keeping an eye on things for him."

"You mean like me?" Richards said.

"No, I doubt Maitland would trust that to you."

"You're probably right," the lawman said. "He doesn't think much of me."

"No, I don't guess he does," Clint said, "but I doubt he thinks much of anyone. Not with his ego."

"What do you think his first move will be once he thinks you're gone?" Richards asked.

"We're going to find out."

Chapter Twenty-Three

Clint spent the night in the jail with Sheriff Richards, but was in the lobby of the hotel the next morning, checking out. After that he bought Richards breakfast. They were served by Newly, and Clint made sure he told the young man he was leaving town.

"Will you be comin' back, Mr. Adams?" Newly asked.

"I don't know, son. Maybe not."

"What about Andy? Ain't you gonna find out who killed him?" Newly asked.

"I think I'm going to leave that to the sheriff."

"The sheriff?" Newly asked.

"What's wrong with me?" Richards asked.

"Nothin', Sheriff," Newly said, "Nothin's wrong." Newly went into the kitchen.

"Whataya gonna do after breakfast?" Richards asked.

"I'll stop in the Bonnet to see Mary and let her know I'm leaving. Then I'll get my horse from the livery and get out of town."

"And what do I do?"

"You just wait. When Maitland comes to town, he's going to ask you where I am."

"And I'm gonna say?"

"All you know is I checked out of the hotel and rode out of town."

"Got it."

"Listen good, Sheriff," Clint said. "If I find out you told Maitland what I planned, I'll come back and see you. Understand?"

"Come back and see me," Richards repeated. "I understand."

"Now you go back to your office. I'll see you when this is all over."

"Sure, Adams, sure."

They both left the dining room. Clint went up to his room while the sheriff left and crossed to his office.

Clint collected his saddlebags and rifle and came down to the desk.

"I'm checking out," Clint said.

"Yes, sir," the clerk said. "That'll be nine dollars."

Clint paid the bill.

"Thanks."

As Clint walked across the lobby, Newly rushed to the doorway of the dining room.

"I hope you come back, Mr. Adams."

"We'll see, Newly, we'll see."

Clint left the hotel and walked to the livery stable.

"I need my horse," he said to the hostler.

"Takin' a ride?" the old man asked,

"Leaving town."

"I'll bring 'im out."

"Fine."

Clint waited while the hostler saddled the Tobiano and brought him out. Clint tossed the saddlebags over the back and slid the rifle home. Then he walked with the horse to the Blue Bonnet. It wasn't open yet, so he knocked on the door. Max opened it and let him in.

"What's goin' on?" he asked.

"I'm leaving town."

"Now?"

"As soon as I talk to Mary."

"She's in her room," Max said. "Probably asleep."

"Should I let her sleep?"

"Uh, no, she'll want to say goodbye."

"Okay, then."

"Coffee when you come down?"

"No, thanks."

Clint went up the stairs and knocked on Mary's door.

"This better be good—" she started, as she opened the door. "Clint!"

"I'll just be a minute," Clint said. "I'm leaving town."

"Leaving?" she asked, pulling her robe closed. "Do you know who killed Andy?"

"No," Clint said, "but I'm tired of hanging around here."

"Are you afraid of this Carrington?" she asked.

"No," he said.

"If you leave, Maitland will come in and take over."

"Only if you sell to him," Clint said.

"He'll make me sell."

"Lean on Max."

"He won't hesitate to kill Max."

"I can't stay around here forever, Mary."

"Clint, you're abandoning me," she said. "Andy was gonna abandon me."

"I can't stay, Mary," he said. "I'm sorry."

"You left Andy here to die, and now you're doing the same thing to me."

"You'll probably only get killed if you refuse to sell," Clint said. "I'm sorry."

"You bastard!"

He turned and went down the stairs.

"So long, Max," he said, as he went out the batwing doors.

Max went to the door and watched Clint mount up. Mary was charging angrily down the stairs, her robe flapping open.

"Gimme that shotgun, Max!" she shouted. "I'm gonna kill that bastard!"

"Forget it, Mary," Max said. "He's already too far for a shotgun to do any good."

They both stood in the doorway and watched Clint ride away.

Chapter Twenty-Four

Clint rode out of town to the east, deliberately away from the Maitland ranch. But after a few miles, he turned back, circled around Bent Fork, and headed for the ranch.

Right after he left town, the old hostler hitched up his buckboard and drove it out to the Maitland ranch. As he approached the house, Tom Finn moved to meet him at the house.

"What brings you here, Tracy?"

"I thought Mr. Maitland would wanna know that Clint Adams left town."

"What? When?"

"This mornin'."

"Headin' where?"

"East."

"Alone?"

"Yup."

"He say where he was goin'?"

"No, he just seemed to be tired of hangin' around Bent Fork."

"Okay, wait here Tracy, while I talk to the boss."

"Awright." Tracy just stood beside the buckboard to wait.

Finn went into the house and found Maitland sitting in the front room, smoking a cigar.

"Boss, the hostler just came with some news."

"What's goin' on?" Maitland asked.

"Adams rode out of town," Finn said,

"For how long?"

"Looks like for good."

"He say that?"

"That's the impression Tracy got."

Maitland twirled his cigar between his lips while he thought.

"You go back to town with Tracy and ask around. I want to know if Adams is gone."

"Should I talk to the sheriff?"

"The sheriff, the bartenders, the waiters, see what everybody says."

"Right."

"And give Tracy fifty dollars."

"Yes, sir."

As Finn turned to leave, Maitland said, "And be back by tonight."

"Yes, sir."

When Finn got outside he told Tracy, "I'm headin' back with ya."

"Suits me. Am I gettin' paid?"

"Yeah," Finn said, "twenty dollars."

"I'd prefer twenty-five."

"You got it, Tracy."

As he climbed back on his buckboard he muttered, "I probably coulda got thirty."

"Meet me by the barn," Finn said, and started walking over.

***

Clint saw the hostler drive his buckboard to the house, to be met by Finn. When he saw the foreman ride back to town with the old man, he knew Tracy had brought the word to Maitland that Clint had left. Now Maitland was sending Finn to town to double check. Clint figured Finn would be able to ask all the questions he needed by nightfall and get back with the news.

He fell in behind them and followed them all the way to town without being seen. Once Finn and the hostler were in town, he needed to find a place to camp.

He chose a clearing between Bent Fork and the ranch. He kept a cold camp so nobody would run into him by accident.

***

Tom Finn split from the hostler as they rode into town. Tracy drove to the livery, while Finn rode to the sheriff's office. He tied his horse off in front and entered.

"What brings you to town, Tom?" Richards asked.

"I heard Clint Adams left," Finn said. "Is that true?"

"He rode out, all right."

"For good?"

"Looks like it."

"Got any reason to think he'll come back?" Finn asked.

"Nope."

"Well," Finn said, "I guess I'll ask around some."

"Be my guest," the sheriff said.

Finn nodded and left.

***

He stopped at the Blue Bonnet and the Lucky Lady and talked to both bartenders. Max confirmed that Clint had left town. The barman at the Lady didn't know. He stopped at the Webster Hotel, found out that Clint had checked out and settled his bill. And he found out from Newly that Clint was gone.

He mounted his horse in front of the hotel and rode out after dark. He knew the way well enough that the dark woudn't be a problem.

***

It was after dark when Clint heard a horse heading out of Bent Fork, past his camp and to the ranch. Figuring it was Finn, Clint broke his cold camp and rode after him. He tailed him back to the ranch and watched from cover.

Chapter Twenty-Five

Finn stood in front of Maitland in the front room and made his report.

"The word I got from everyone—the sheriff, the bartenders, some others at the hotel—is that Adams checked out, paid his bill, and left."

"I didn't think I'd be able to wait him out," Maitland said, "but it's just as well. This way I'm done with Saxon and Adams."

"So what's next?" Finn asked.

"I'll go to town and take another run at Mary Ward," Maitland said.

"Want me to go with you, Mr. Maitland?"

"No," Maitland said, "I'll take Carrington with me."

"With Adams gone you think you'll need Carrington?"

"He won't need to do anything but stand there," Maitland said. "You just stay here and do your job. Start by getting my buggy hitched up and brought to the front in the morning, along with Carrington."

"Yes, sir."

Finn left to arrange for the buggy.

***

When Maitland came out the front door in the morning, Carrington was standing there with the buggy.

"It's about time we're goin' somewhere," Carrington said.

"Adams left town yesterday," Maitland said, "so it's time for us to go to the Blue Bonnet, again."

As Maitland climbed aboard his buggy and Carrington mounted his horse, the gunman said, "The first thing you've got to do is change the name of that place."

They headed for town.

***

Clint watched as Maitland and Carrington left the ranch and headed for Bent Fork. Maitland wasn't wasting any time. Clint mounted his Tobiano, and headed out after them, being careful not to get too close.

He watched from a distance as they rode down Trail Street.

***

They reined in their horses in front of The Blue Bonnet and stepped down.

"Do you understand your role?" Maitland asked.

"Yeah, I'm the big, scary gunman."

"And that's all you have to do or be, unless somebody tries to make a play with a gun."

"Like the girl?" Carrington asked.

"She hates guns," Maitland said. "Under no circumstances is she to be killed, understand?"

"What about that big bartender?" Carrington asked. "He's bound to have a rifle or a shotgun behind the bar."

"If he produces a shotgun," Maitland said, "he'll be asking for it."

"And?"

"And you kill him."

They mounted the boardwalk and entered the saloon.

***

It was early afternoon. The Bonnet had just opened and there were not yet any customers. Max watched as Maitland and Carrington approached the bar.

" 'mornin', gents," he said. "What can I do for you?"

"I'd like to talk to Miss Ward," Maitland said.

"She told you she never wanted to speak to you again," Max said.

"That was before."

"Before what?"

"Before Adams came and went," Maitland said. "Now we start over." He looked up. "Is she in her room?"

"Look here—" Max started.

"I'm going to leave Mr. Carrington here with you, Max. Be good and just stand there."

Maitland walked to the stairs and started up. Max moved his hand beneath the bar, but Carrington drew his gun and slapped it down.

"Don't even think about it." Max pulled his hand back up. "Just get me a beer."

"Yeah, sure."

Maitland went up the stairs and knocked on Mary's door.

"Clint—" she said, opening the door. When she saw Maitland she stopped short, then said, "You!" and tried to slam the door.

"Take it easy," he said, stopping the door with the flat of his hand. "I just want to talk."

She backed away, and as he entered she said, "Leave the door open."

"Of course."

Mary walked across the room, then turned to face him with her arms crossed.

"What do you want now, Maitland?" she demanded.

Chapter Twenty-Six

"We've talked about this before, Miss Ward," Maitland said. "With Saxon and Adams both gone, just sell and be on your way."

"On my way where?" she asked. "This is my home."

"Okay, then sell to me and I'll hire you to run the place. Nothing has to change."

"Everything has to change," she said. "Now get out of here before I kill you."

"You haven't even heard my latest offer."

"Get . . . out!" she screamed.

Calmly, Maitland said, "All right, as you wish. I'll give you the rest of the day to make up your mind. Then if you don't sell to me, I'll take the place."

"Maitland—"

"I know," the rancher said, "get out or you'll kill me. Remember, the rest of the day. That's until closing time. Get it?"

She gritted her teeth and said, "I get it."

Maitland turned and left her room. She hurried to the door and slammed it, then put her back against it.

***

When Maitland got back to the bar Max put two more beers out for them.

"She turn you down?" he asked.

"For now," Maitland said. "She's got until closing to change her mind."

Maitland and Carrington drank their beers and put the mugs down.

"What about him?" Carrington asked, indicating Max.

"You're just in the mood to kill somebody, aren't you?" the bartender asked.

"Don't worry, Carrington," Maitland said, "your time will come."

"So where do we go from here?" the gunman asked.

"Let's spend some time at the Cattleman's Club."

"They gonna let us is there?" Carrington said. "You don't even have any cattle, yet."

"That's going to change," Maitland said, "real soon."

***

After Maitland and Carrington left, Mary came down to the bar.

"He make another offer now that Clint Adams is gone?" Max asked.

"Yes. I turned him down, but I don't think he's going to take no for an answer."

"I wouldn't think so."

"The only way we might keep the place is to sell it to him, but work for him."

"I don't like the way that sounds," Max said.

"Neither do I."

"Let's see what happens."

"We only got til the end of the day, Max," Mary said. "I don't know what can happen by then."

She turned and went back up to her room.

***

Clint watched from cover while Maitland and Carrington went into the Blue Bonnet. Before long they came out again. They took their horse and carriage to the livery, then went to a building Clint eventually discovered housed the Cattleman's Club. He hadn't seen any cattle on Maitland's property, but that didn't stop them from being let in. He probably had big plans.

Clint was satisfied to have Maitland and Carrington in the club. He didn't have to worry about them while they were in there.

He had left his Tobiano behind the livery, where nobody would see it. Now he walked back to it and stroked his neck.

"Toby, you're the only one I can trust, these days," he said. "I've been making some bad decisions, lately, like the one that got Andy Saxon killed. But what's the truth? If I had stayed to help Andy, would he have picked up his gun, or would he have left all the gunplay to me? And in that case, would he have gotten killed, anyway?

There were a lot of questions ahead of him. Not only what he has going to do about things in Bent Fork, but things in the rest of his life. Life was moving towards a new century, and things were going to change. Was he going to change with the times? And how? It was a forgone conclusion that he could not take his gun off. The way to change was not to give up his gun, but to use it less.

"Big boy, after this you and me are going to travel, stay on the trail a while, relax, maybe even find us a place where I can take the gun off for a while." He ruffled the Tobiano's mane. "I wonder what that would be like, huh?"

He would have liked to take the saddle off the Tobiano, rub him down and give him some feed but he didn't know when he would have to ride him again.

Chapter Twenty-Seven

Carrington was halfway through his steak before he looked up from his plate.

"You ain't talkin' or eatin'," Carrington said. "What's on your mind?"

"I'm not sure I'm buying that Adams left town," Maitland said. "The more I think about it, the less sense it makes."

"It never sat right with me, either. It just doesn't seem his way."

"So then he's around here somewhere, watching," Maitland commented.

"And waiting," Carrington said. "If you don't eat that, he'll know you've got somethin' on your mind."

"That's a good point," Maitland said. He picked up his utensils, cut a hunk from his steak and put it in his mouth. He chewed thoughtfully. "I think I might have made a wrong move going to see Mary Ward so quickly."

"Do you think anybody doesn't know you're after her place?" Carrington asked.

"Probably not."

"Then he's probably watchin' right now."

"I doubt he's anywhere in here," Maitland said, putting his fork down. "But he's probably outside."

"Then let him watch," Carrington said. "Let's finish our meals, and you can plan your next move."

***

Although everyone in town believed that Clint had left, he felt that either Maitland, Carrington or both hadn't bought the ruse once they thought it over.

The chances were good that Maitland and Carrington would head back to the ranch. Clint decided to wait for them to come out and see what their reaction would be. He walked back to the Cattleman's Club and climbed aboard Maitland's carriage to wait.

***

"What's the plan?" Carrington asked, pushing his plate away.

"I feel I've been sucked into the Gunsmith's plan. I should've brought more men."

"If Adams is really gone, it doesn't matter, but we'll have to decide."

"If he's still here, I can get rid of him," Carrington said.

"Do you really think you can take him?"

"I'm younger and stronger," Carrington said.

"But are you faster?"

"It isn't always the one who's faster but who comes out on top," Carrington said. "It's who shoots straighter."

"Well, don't try it until I say so."

"The only time I'll try it is when the right opportunity presents itself."

"If you try it before I say so," Maitland said, "you'll be playing right into his hands."

"Then haven't we already done that by comin' to town?" Carrington asked.

"I'm afraid so," Maitland said. "Let's get back to the ranch and wait for him to come to us."

"Now?"

"No," Maitland said, "if he is in town and watching, let's make him watch longer. Pie?"

***

They stood and walked to the front door sometime later. As they exited, Maitland saw Clint sitting in his carriage. He was still there, despite the fact that he had started to become impatient.

"Looks like this is it," Carrington said. "There's a nice audience—or there will be."

"Adams," Maitland said. "I knew you didn't leave."

"A bad plan on my part, Maitland," Clint admitted, dropping down from the carriage seat. "Hello, Carrington. Are you ready?"

"Not yet, Carrington," Maitland said. "Make him wait for it."

"I thought you were your own man, Carrington," Clint said.

"Leave that gun in your holster, Carrington, and let's go."

"Your strategy didn't work, Adams. Try again."

"I'll be trying until I find out you had Andy Saxon killed."

"I didn't kill Saxon, or have him killed."

Clint looked at Carrington.

"He was shot in the back," Carrington said. "I didn't do it."

Maitland walked to his carriage and climbed into the seat. Carrington walked slowly to his horse and mounted up. They both turned and rode up Trail Street, and out of town.

***

Clint felt foolish while checking back into the Webster Hotel.

"You're back, sir," the clerk said. "The same room?"

"No, the one across from it."

"As you wish." The clerk handed him a key. "Welcome back," he said.

"I wish I had another choice," Clint said.

When he got to his room he washed up, changed into clean clothes and went back down to the dining room. He had already put his horse back in the livery.

When he walked in Newly stopped him right away.

"You came back!" he said, happily. "I hoped, but I didn't expect you so soon."

"My plan was ill-advised," Clint said.

"Well, have a seat and I'll bring you a good meal."

Clint sat to wait and think.

Chapter Twenty-Eight

Newly brought Clint a bowl of thick, succulent stew and a bowl of biscuits. While he was eating, Sheriff Richards came in and approached his table.

"You're back," the lawman said.

"So they tell me," Clint said. "Who told you?"

"The hostler."

"Have a seat, then, and a cup of coffee."

"Thanks." Richards sat down and Newly brought him a cup of coffee. "Maitland was in town with his top gun."

"I know. I spoke with them."

"And no one died?"

"Not today."

"Then when?"

"There's no way to know that," Clint said. "Maitland seems to have a tight rein on Carrington."

"And when will he loosen that rein?" the lawman asked.

"At a time of his own choosing," Clint said. "When he feels I'm ready to be taken."

"Why don't you take him, first?"

"That may be what I decide to do."

"And when will you make up your mind?" Richards asked.

Clint continued to eat as he spoke.

"Maitland stopped in to see Mary Ward. I want to find out what he said to her. Maybe then I'll make up my mind."

"If you're convinced Maitland had Carrington kill Saxon, why not just take care of them?"

"Because I'm not convinced," Clint said. He pushed his plate away. "Come on, take a walk with me."

Richards followed him out.

***

"Where's the spot?" Clint asked Richards a bit later.

"What spot?" the lawman asked.

"Where Saxon was when he got shot."

"Down the street," the lawman said. "He was walkin' across, after leavin' the Bonnet."

They walked down the street and stopped.

"I found him lying in the middle of the street," Richards said.

"Was Maitland in town when it happened?"

"I don't know," Richards said.

"What about Carrington?"

"I don't know that, either."

"You didn't see either one of them?"

"No."

"Did you ask them where they were?" Clint asked.

"I did," Richards said. "They both said they were at the ranch."

Clint stood in the middle of the street and looked around. There were many vantage points from where Saxon could have been shot.

"Okay," Clint said, "you might as well go back to your office."

"Where are you goin'?"

"The Blue Bonnet, to talk to Mary Ward again," Clint said. "After that, I don't know."

"You don't want nothin' else from me?" the lawman asked.

"Nothing."

Sheriff Richards remained in the middle of the street, looking lost, while Clint walked to the Blue Bonnet.

***

Max looked up from serving a customer and saw Clint approaching the bar. He walked down and met Clint at the halfway point in the bar.

"Why doesn't this surprise me?" the bartender asked.

"You didn't believe I was gone?" Clint asked.

"You never struck me as the kind of man who would walk away from this," Max said. "Mary needs you, but you also need to finish this."

"Yes, I'm afraid I do need to."

"You want a beer while you wait?" Max asked,

"Sure," Clint said, "but I'm not going to wait long."

Max drew a cold beer and set it in front of him.

"You have to talk to Mary," Max said. "Last time I saw her, she wanted to kill you."

"I know," Clint said. "It was a bad plan."

"She's upstairs."

Clint picked up his beer, drained it, set the mug down on the bar, then walked to the stairs. As he walked up, he remembered the look on Mary's face the last time he saw her. When he reached the door he knocked and waited.

"Go away!" she shouted from inside. "Whoever it is!"

"Mary. It's Clint," he called out. "Open up."

The door swiftly swung open.

"What do you want to tell me now?" she demanded.

"I made a mistake," Clint said. "I pretended to leave, but it didn't work. I'm not going to leave until I find out who killed Andy."

Chapter Twenty-Nine

Clint hadn't expected it, but they ended up in bed, bucking wildly against each other until they were both exhausted.

Eventually, they laid in each other's arms, getting their breath back.

"What are you gonna do now?" she asked. "Leave again?"

"I never left," he said, "and I'm not going to leave now. Not til I find out who killed Andy."

"What about who shot at me?" she asked.

"Yes, that, too," he agreed. "I suspect it's the same person."

"Maitland!"

"I doubt he did any shooting, himself," Clint said. "But somebody might have done it for him."

"One of his gunmen."

"Probably."

"I should've killed Maitland myself when he came here again."

"If you did that, you'd be in jail."

"I would've said it was self-defense."

"Did he have a gun?"

"I don't know, but I'd say he did."

"Mary, just leave this to me."

"When are you gonna get it done?" she asked.

"I don't know, but I hope soon."

"What about this gunman, Carrington?"

"It might come down to him and me," Clint said. "We'll have to wait and see."

"I'm so tired of waiting," she complained.

"I understand."

"There's only one way I can work off this impatience."

He thought he knew what she meant, and she proved his point the next moment by grabbing his semi-hard cock. "I need this!"

She slid down between his legs and took his cock into her mouth. She sucked it avidly until it was fully hard, then released it from her mouth, gleaming from her spit, so she could shinny up on him and slide it deep into her. Once again, they went at each other, with Clint doing his best to match her desperate tempo . . .

***

Mary reclined, still naked, on the bed and watched him dress.

"Why don't you just kill Carrington, so Maitland doesn't have him to call on?" she demanded.

"I can't kill the man just so Maitland has to find somebody else," Clint said. "Once I know Carrington pulled the trigger on Andy, it'll be different."

"I have to say, both you and Andy haven't lived up to your reputations."

"Most reputations are a bunch of bull crap. And more men get killed just trying to live up to them."

"I'd like to see this fella Carrington try to live up to his," Mary said. "And, hopefully, a stray bullet would kill Maitland."

"That may all happen, Mary," Clint said. "But I recommend you stay inside for the time being."

"As long as you promise me you're not leaving town, or even pretending to."

"I'm going to be here until I find out who killed Andy, and I see that he pays for it."

"I don't like the idea of goin' into hidin', but I'll do what you say . . . for now. Will you be coming back here?"

"I'll be staying at my hotel, but I will be coming back to, uh, see you."

"Then I'll keep myself ready for you," she said, tossing the sheet back to reveal her nude glory.

He got out of there quickly.

***

Since he had been with Mary in her room for some time, Max had a good idea what had gone on.

"You look like you need a beer," Max said, putting one on the bar.

"I could use one," Clint agreed, picking it up.

"I guess you convinced her not to kill you," Max said.

"It took some time, but yes, I did," Clint said. "And I think I have her convinced to stay inside until this is all over." Clint finished the beer and said, "Thanks. I'll be in my hotel, Max."

"I'll keep an eye on her."

Clint left and walked back to his hotel, keeping alert for a possible ambush. This had all been taking much too long. When he got to his room, he removed his boots and hung his gunbelt on the bedpost. Then he sat on the bed and gave the matter some thought. Remembering what Mary had said about his reputation. As he got older, he certainly was not the man he had once been. There was a time he might have pushed Carrington into a play so he could kill him. Those were the days that even he believed in his own reputation. He didn't like killing, but he could still do it when it was called for. Perhaps he should have been pushing a little harder . . .

***

In pretending to leave town Clint had been on the move, so he put off any further moves until the next morning.

There was no access to his room from the window, so he only had to worry about the door. He shoved a straight-backed wooden chair under the doorknob, and went to sleep.

He woke early the next morning, feeling refreshed, and ready to make a more indelible impression on Maitland and Carrington.

He had his usual breakfast in a mostly empty dining room, served by Newly.

"Have you made any progress, Mr. Adams?" he asked.

"Yes," Clint said, "I've decided not to be such a nice guy."

"You gonna kill somebody?"

"If I have to," Clint replied.

"I hope I get to see you go against Del Carrington," Newly said. "You'll out draw him clean, I'll bet."

"We might find out."

"You think he might be faster than you?"

"There's always going to be somebody faster, Newly. We'll have to wait and see."

"Wow, if you believe that, aren't you scared every time you go up against somebody?"

"You bet I am."

Chapter Thirty

Maitland found Carrington at the corral, watching a couple of hands working the stock.

"Nice animals," Carrington said.

"What do you know about horses?"

"Enough to ride one," Carrington said.

"I thought so. I didn't hire you for your knowledge of horses."

"I'm starting to wonder what you hired me for," Carrington said.

"Maybe you'll find out today," Maitland said. "I want you to go to town."

"And do what?"

"From now on, Carrington, I want you to do whatever you have to do."

"Make my own decisions?"

Maitland nodded.

"Your own decisions."

***

Clint found Sheriff Richards behind his desk in his office.

"What brings you in, Mr. Adams?" Richards asked.

"I want some information."

"About what?"

"I know Maitland's got Del Carrington on his pay-roll," Clint said. "And his foreman, Tom Finn. How many other men does he employ, and how many of them are gunmen."

"He's got about fifteen hands on his place, but he's still growing it," Richards explained. "As for how many are gunmen, they're all hands, but they all wear guns. I guess that means I don't know the answer."

"So any one of those men could have shot Andy Saxon."

"I suppose that's true," Richards said, "but it was most likely Carrington. You gonna try 'im?"

"Only if I have to," Clint said. "I'm going to push Maitland and see if I can get him to talk."

"What if he's got nothing to talk about?" Richards asked.

"You mean like he's got nothing to do with it?" Clint asked.

"Could be, couldn't it?"

"Sure," Clint said, "could even be that you killed Andy."

Richards' face fell.

"That ain't funny."

"I'm just saying, anything could be true."

"Not that, believe me," the lawman said.

"I was just saying."

"What are you gonna do now?"

"Like I said, I'm going to push Maitland."

"Push him into a fight?"

"No," Clint said, "I just want him to talk, and say something wrong, something I can use to nail him."

"You might push him into sending Carrington after you," the lawman offered.

"If that happens, it happens," Clint said. "I just want to find out, once and for all, if Maitland was responsible for Andy Saxon's death."

"I'd like this whole thing to come to an end, too," Richards said.

"What can you tell me about the men on the Maitland ranch?" Clint asked. "Anybody there who might have taken the job to shoot Saxon in the back?"

"If they were offered enough money, sure. But I still say Carrington's the best bet."

"I'm going to operate on that assumption," Clint said. "Carrington tried to convince me he had a code of ethics, but I don't think so."

"What do you want me to do?" Richards asked.

"Just your job. Make your rounds as you normally will. I'll keep in touch."

With no further word, Clint turned and left. Richards hoped the Gunsmith was actually going to get some results.

***

Clint was surprised while walking away from the sheriff's office, to see Del Carrington riding into town. He stopped in front of the Lucky Lady and waited for the rider to reach him.

" 'mornin', Adams," Carrington said.

"Carrington," Clint said. "What brings you back to town so soon?"

"The boss sent me in," the gunman said. "Said I was on my own today."

"No specific orders?"

Carrington shook his head.

"I haven't been told what to do or not to do," the man said. "I'm on my own."

"Have any plans?"

"Nothin' specific," Carrington said. "I'll start by out-ing my horse in the livery, and then go from there. Maybe we can have a beer later."

"Maybe we can," Clint said.

Carrington was very relaxed as he rode toward the livery stable.

Chapter Thirty-One

Clint remained in front of the Lucky Lady, which hadn't opened yet. He took a moment to wonder what Maitland's intention was in sending Carrington to town on his own. If it was to set-up a showdown between the two, then maybe he should stop avoiding it, and welcome it as an opportunity to make a statement to Maitland by getting rid of his top gun. But as much as he was thinking he should probably take a more active role, he still thought he would let Carrington call the play. As many gunfights as he had taken part in over the years, he still preferred not to be the one to call the play. His reputation was for coming out on top in a gunfight, not for causing them. There were enough gunmen throughout the West who deliberately picked fights with lesser skilled men.

So his decision was to see what decision Del Carrington was going to make.

He moved away from the Lucky Lady, not wanting to give Maitland's saloon any of his business, and headed for the Blue Bonnet.

***

After dispatching Del Carrington to Bent Fork, Maitland called his foreman, Tom Finn, over to him. They both stood, leaning on the corral.

"Who are our three best guns?" he asked the foreman.

"Best hands, or best guns?" Finn asked.

"Guns, Tom," Maitland said. "I'll worry about hiring good hands when my business in town is wrapped up."

Finn knew this meant after Maitland had successfully wrested The Blue Bonnet away from Mary Ward.

"Well, there's—"

"Never mind," Maitland said. "Their names don't matter. Just send them up to me at the house."

"When, sir?"

"Now!"

Maitland turned and walked to the house.

Finn did some quick figuring, then went to find the three men he figured were the best they had.

***

Maitland received the three men in the front room, after watching through the window as they approached.

"You men understand you were never hired for your skills as cowhands, right?"

"Yes, Sir," one of them said.

"Good. You all know that the Gunsmith is in Bent Fork, don't you?"

"Yes, Sir," another said.

"Do any of you have doubts about facing him?"

The three men exchanged glances, and then the spokesman said, "No, Sir, we don't, but—"

"But what?"

"What about Carrington?"

"I'm sending you in as back-up," Maitland said. "If Carrington doesn't get the job done, you will."

"And?"

"And what?"

"We'll be paid what Carrington's gettin' paid?" the man asked.

"If Carrington doesn't get the job done, you three will split his pay."

The three men exchanged another glance.

"Each," the man said.

"What?"

"We'll each get what Carrington was gonna get."

"Each?" Maitland repeated.

"Each," the spokesman said.

Maitland waited a moment, then said, "Very well. You'll each get what Carrington would've gotten, if you get the job done."

"If we don't get the job done, it won't matter."

"Indeed," Maitland said.

***

Maitland watched from the porch as the three men walked their horses out of the barn, mounted up and rode off.

Tom Finn came up to the porch.

"Are you finally makin' a push?" he asked.

"Yes," Maitland said, "I'm tired of waiting."

"You want me to go to town?" Finn asked.

"What for?" Maitland asked. "I didn't hire you for your gun."

As Finn started for the barn, Maitland called out, "And remember, I'm going to need you to run this place when I'm running things in town."

"Yes, Sir," Finn said.

Chapter Thirty-Two

Clint entered The Blue Bonnet and bellied up to the bar, even though the place wasn't open, yet.

"Kinda early," Max said. "I don't even think Mary's awake."

"That's okay," Clint said. "I'm not here to see her. Del Carrington's in town, and I don't want him to have any trouble finding me, if he decides to."

"Beer?"

"Coffee'll do," Clint said.

"Comin' up."

Max set a steaming mug of coffee on the bar.

"Thanks," Clint said.

"You figure Carrington's in town to give you something to think about?" Max asked.

"He says he's making his own decisions," Clint said. "So I guess he's going to make his own move."

"So Maitland's givin' him his head," Max said. "He can make up his own mind about facin' you?"

"Looks like it."

"Whataya think he's gonna do?" Max asked.

"He's probably going to pick his spot to make his move," Clint said.

"And you're gonna let 'im? Why?"

"Because it doesn't matter where or when he picks it," Clint said, "I'll be ready for him."

***

Sheriff Richards happened to be looking out his window when the three back-up men from Maitland's ranch rode into town. The lawman recognized the men as Maitland's gunmen, and he assumed the ranch had sent them into town after Clint Adams.

He stepped out of his office to watch as the men rode by, to see where they went. At the same time, he saw Del Carrington walking from the direction of the livery stable. When they encountered each other, they all stopped. The lawman remained where he was and watched with great interest.

***

"What are you men doin' in town?" Carrington asked, staring up at the three mounted riders.

The three gunmen looked down at him and the spokesman—Dolan—said, "Mr. Maitland sent us in."

"For what purpose?" Carrington asked. "Not to back my play, because I don't need back-up."

"Not exactly," Dolan said, "but he did say he wanted us to take a hand if you didn't get the job done."

"All three of you?" Carrington asked.

"That's right."

Carrington didn't like the idea of Clint Adams having to take on three experienced gunmen at one time.

"Well, just make sure you don't take a hand in my play," Carrington said. "Understand?"

"We understand," Dolan said. "We're just gonna put our horses up in the stable, and then get a drink."

"Just understand, don't make a move on Adams before I do," Carrington said.

"And if he kills you?"

Carrington smiled and said, "Then he's all yours, if you think you can take the Gunsmith."

"Deal," Dolan said. He and his cronies rode toward the livery stable.

Carrington started walking.

Richards figured he could take a chance, find Adams and warn him. Or he could just go back into his office and wait for things to play out.

It looked to him like Carrington was heading for The Blue Bonnet Saloon. It was likely that was where he would find the Gunsmith.

Richards chose to go back into his office.

***

Clint was working on a coffee refill when Carrington walked in.

"We ain't open yet—" Max started, but Clint put his hand out.

"Give Mr. Carrington what he wants, on me, Max," Clint said.

"Sure, Mr. Adams," the bartender said.

Carrington came up next to Clint and said, "Thanks."

"Sure," Clint said.

Max put a mug of coffee in front of Carrington, and refilled Clint's.

"Make any decisions yet?" Clint asked.

"Actually, yeah, I have. Turns out Maitland's not all that confident in me."

"What do you mean?"

"Three more men just rode in from Maitland's ranch," Carrington said.

"Did you talk to them?"

"I did," Carrington said. "I told them to make sure they didn't interfere with my play."

"Are they going to wait?"

"They'll wait," Carrington said. "They won't make a move unless you kill me."

"I see. Are they any good?"

"They're pros. But I don't like it."

"Why's that?" Clint asked.

"Three against one," Carrington said. "I don't like the odds."

"What do you care?" Clint asked. "You'd be dead."

"I don't like that idea either," Carrington said. "I don't like the idea of anyone havin' to face three."

"You mean you have a code of ethics?"

"Sure I do. A man like you shouldn't get killed facin' three two-bit guns."

"I thought you said they were pros."

"That just means they sell their guns for money," Carrington said.

"They're not up to your standards?"

"Or yours," Carrington said.

"So what's on your mind?"

"I'm thinkin' maybe we should take care of them, before we face each other."

"You'd go against Maitland's men?"

"Why not? He should've had more faith in me than to send them. Whataya say?"

"Why not?" Clint asked. "I'm tired of holding myself back. You got an idea?"

Carrington nodded and said, "I've got an idea."

Chapter Thirty-Three

Clint listened to Carrington's idea and, although he didn't trust the man one hundred per cent, he agreed to go along with it. They remained at the bar in The Blue Bonnet until the saloon opened and a few more customers came in. They switched from coffee to beer and kept an eye on the three gunmen through the front window.

"You think this will work?" Clint asked.

"It'll work."

"And you're willing to take this all the way?" Clint asked.

"I don't like these men," Carrington said. "They'll deserve what they get. They're bottom feeders."

"Okay, then," Clint said. "Let's see what happens."

***

Dolan and his two partners were getting tired of waiting in doorways across from The Blue Bonnet.

"When's somethin' gonna happen?" one of them complained.

"It'll be today," Dolan said. "We just hafta keep waitin'—" He got cut off by the sound of shots from across the street. "That's it!" he snapped and sprang from the doorway. The other two followed him, as he ran across the street.

When the three men burst through the batwing doors, they saw Carrington standing at the bar with his gun in one hand and a beer in the other.

"You did it," Dolan said. "You killed the Gunsmith."

"Not hardly."

A man came walking from the other end of the bar.

"I'm Adams," Clint said. "Sorry to disappoint you."

"Say, what is this, Carrington?" Dolan asked. "I thought you were gonna kill 'im."

"Well, I was thinkin' about you boys wantin' to do it," Carrington said. "You wanna impress Mr. Maitland?"

"You said you want us to stay away from Adams," Dolan said. "Why did you change your mind?"

"Look," Carrington said, "if and when I want him dead, I'll do it myself, alone."

"So?"

"You three are waitin' to go against him, three-to-one. That's a coward's play. I'd hate to see a man like Clint Adams gunned down by three men."

"What are you gettin' at?" Dolan asked.

"I'm gonna give you the chance," Carrington said. "The three of you against Adams . . . and me."

"What?"

"That's right," Carrington said, "but not three-to-one. I'm gonna make it three-to-two."

Dolan looked at the other two men.

"You're crazy," Dolan said, "but if you wanna play it this way, that's fine." He looked at Clint. "Big man like you needs help?"

"I'm willing to face the three of you myself, but Carrington won't have it. He wants it to be a fair fight."

"Fair?" Dolan said. "Three-to-two?"

Carrington said, "I could take the three of you myself. So could Adams. But if you're gonna do it, you'll have to face the two of us."

The men seated at tables quickly stood, turned their tables over and took cover.

"Adams?" Dolan said, "why don't you let us take Carrington first, and then we'll face you. Whataya care if we kill 'im? He's gonna try to kill you."

"That may be true," Clint said, "but like he said, he's going to do it on his own. You might be looking to make an impression on Maitland, but that's what I'm going to do. I'm going to send the three of you back to him in a gunny sack each."

"And what about Carrington?" Dolan asked.

"You don't have to worry about that, Dolan," Carrington said. "Not at all."

Chapter Thirty-Four

It got very quiet in the saloon.

"I suggest we take this outside," Clint said.

"Suits me," Carrington said.

"Me, too," Max said, but nobody paid attention to him.

Moving together, Clint and Carrington carefully moved towards the door. The three gunmen had the choice of backing out or moving aside. They chose to back out.

When they were all in the street everyone inside rushed to the windows. Max came around from behind the bar and rushed to the batwing doors.

The five men spread out on the street, which had already emptied in anticipation of trouble.

Dolan and his two compadres spread out a good arm's length apart from each other.

Clint and Carrington were close enough to talk.

"Dolan's the one to watch," Carrington said. "You want me to take 'im?"

"If you want him," Clint said, "I'll take the other two."

"Dolan's in the middle."

"No problem," Clint said. "You just concentrate on Dolan."

"Come on, Dolan," Carrington called out. "Call the play."

"You're crazy, Del," Dolan said.

"Walk away, Dolan," Clint said. "The three of you can get on your horses and ride."

"We got a job to do," Dolan said. "Let's get it done."

"Call it, Dolan!" Carrington shouted.

Carrington's shout urged Dolan into action. Clint could see that Carrington was right. They might have been pros, but they weren't fast. Carrington put one in Dolan's chest easily. Clint fired twice before either of the other men cleared leather.

They walked to the bodies and checked them and confirmed that they were all dead. Some of the customers stepped out of the saloon for a look. Clint glanced around. As a small crowd gathered, he didn't see the sheriff.

Clint ejected the spent shells from his gun, reloaded and holstered it. Carrington followed. By this time the sheriff finally arrived.

"Surprised to see us both alive?" Carrington asked.

"I'm surprised to see you standin' over Maitland's men," Richards said, "and with Clint Adams."

"The three of them were gonna try to gun down Adams," Carrington said. "I couldn't watch that. A man like Clint Adams shouldn't be killed by three two-bit gunnies." He looked at Clint. "I'm gonna have a drink. Join me?"

"In a minute."

Carrington walked to the saloon door and everybody moved out of his way.

"What was this about?" Sheriff Richards asked.

"I think what Carrington said was partially true," Clint said.

"Partially? Why would he kill some of Maitland's men?"

"I think he wanted to see me in action," Clint said. "If he's going to make a play, he'd want to watch me work."

"You might be right," Richards said, looking around. "I'll get some men to take these bodies to the undertaker."

"I have an idea," Clint said. "Can you send someone out to give Maitland the news?"

"That his men are dead?"

"And that Carrington and I are both still alive."

"Okay. I'll send someone."

"I'll go inside and have a drink with Carrington," Clint said.

"Do you think he'll try you today?" Richards asked.

"I don't think so," Clint said. "I think he'll want to digest what he saw."

"I hope you're right."

As Clint started for the saloon, the sheriff asked, "What about what you saw, Mr. Adams?"

Clint turned and said, "He's fast, awful fast, but more than that, he's steady."

He went into the saloon.

***

At the sound of the shots Mary Ward ran from her room to the front of the second floor, to look out the window. She saw the bodies in the street, and Clint and Carrington standing over them. Satisfied that Clint was unhurt, she returned to her room.

***

The tables had been turned upright, and the patrons had reseated themselves. They all had fresh drinks.

Clint joined Carrington at the bar.

"I stood drinks for the house," he told Clint. "And one for you."

Clint picked up the beer and said, "Thanks."

"You have a helluva move," Carrington said. "Neither of them cleared leather."

"You were pretty fast, yourself," Clint said.

"I was hoping you noticed."

Chapter Thirty-Five

Instead of sending someone to Maitland's ranch to give him the news, Sheriff Richards went there himself. After clearing the bodies off the street, he saddled his horse and rode out. Tom Finn was watching one of the hands working a horse in the corral when Richards approached.

The lawman saw Finn at the corral and rode over there. Finn saw him approaching and turned to face him.

"What are you doin' here?" he demanded. "The boss told you never to come out here."

"I got news he's gonna be interested in," Richards told Finn. "Where is he?"

"In his office," Finn said. "He don't like being interrupted when he's doin' paperwork."

"Believe me, he's gonna be interested in this," the lawman said.

"You better be right," Finn said. "Come with me. Leave your horse here." Finn waved at one of the men to take care of the sheriff's animal.

The two men walked to the house, with Finn leading the way.

Finn opened the front door and led the way in. When they reached the office Finn recalled how Carrington had barged past him. He turned and put his hand on Richards' chest.

"Wait here!" he snapped.

He entered the office, and Maitland looked up from his desk.

"What are you doing here?" he demanded of his foreman.

"The sheriff's here, claims he's got somethin' real important to tell you."

"Where is he?"

"In the hall."

Maitland scowled and sat back in his chair.

"All right, bring him in."

"Yes, Sir."

Finn stepped into the hall and said, "Go on in."

Richards entered the office with Finn behind him.

"Mr. Maitland—" the lawman started.

"This better be good, Sheriff."

"I thought you'd wanna know there was a shootin' in town," Richards said.

"Who's dead, the Gunsmith or Carrington?" Maitland asked.

"Neither one," Richards said. "Did you send three other men to town?"

"I did."

"Well, they're dead."

"All three?" Maitland asked.

"Yes."

"Did Adams kill them?"

"Adams and Carrington."

"What? Carrington killed my men?" Maitland said.

"Yes, Sir."

"What the hell—did he say why he did that?"

"He didn't want to see Adams face three men alone."

"So they stood together?"

"Yes, Sir."

"Why would Adams stand with Carrington?" Maitland said.

"According to Adams, he thinks Carrington wanted to see his move before he took a chance on facin' him," the lawman said.

Maitland thought that over and then said, "That may have been a smart move. You think Carrington will still face him after seeing that?"

"Hell, I dunno," Richards said. "I guess that depends on how good Carrington really thinks he is."

"He thinks he's the best," Maitland said. "That's why I hired him."

"Well, whataya want me to do?" Richards asked.

"I want you to stay out of the way," Maitland said. "Just let Carrington do what I hired him to do."

"What about Mary Ward?" Richards asked.

"What about her?"

"Is Carrington gonna kill her?"

"He's going to do what he thinks he has to do," Maitland said. "You just go back to town and stay out of the way."

"Yes, Sir."

"Wait at the end of the hall for Finn," Maitland said.

"Yes, Sir."

Richards left the office and Finn stepped up to the desk.

"You think Carrington's gonna get it done?" Finn asked.

"Obviously," Maitland said, "I didn't send enough men to town."

"You want me to send more?"

"Yeah," Maitland said, "but I don't know how many more. Get about a dozen of them ready, and let's see what Carrington does."

"A dozen?"

"Not enough?" Maitland asked.

"Yes—I mean, no—I mean . . . we don't have a dozen more guns," Finn said. "I'll have to ask some of our cowhands to strap on guns."

"We just need a show of force," Maitland said. "I don't think even the Gunsmith will outshoot a dozen guns."

"So I can tell 'em we really don't want them to go against the Gunsmith?"

"You gather them in front of the barn," Maitland said. "I'll come out and talk to them."

"Yes, sir."

Finn started away, but Maitland called him back.

"Finn!"

"Yes, Sir."

"Make sure the sheriff leaves, first."

"Yes, Sir."

Maitland waved and said, "Go."

***

Outside, Finn walked the sheriff to his horse.

"What's he want me to do?" Richards asked.

"Just get back to town and do nothin'."

"Nothin'?"

"Just watch and do nothin'," Finn said. "Can you do that?"

"I can do that."

"Then go."

The lawman mounted up and headed back to Bent Fork.

Finn looked around and started choosing men.

Chapter Thirty-Six

Clint saw Mary Ward appear at the top of the steps and wave to Max, then go back into her room. Max moved to the far end of the bar and beckoned to Clint.

"Looks like somebody's callin' you," Carrington said.

Clint didn't respond, and walked over to where Max was.

"She wants to talk to you," Max said.

"Then I guess I better see what the lady wants," Clint said.

Max didn't look happy when he said, "I think you know what the lady wants."

"I'll be right back," Clint said.

As he walked to the stairs and up, he could feel Carrington's eyes on him. He wondered when the gunman would make up his mind about his next move.

When he knocked on Mary's door she snapped, "Come!"

He opened the door and entered. He didn't know what to expect, but she looked as if she was dressed for riding—trousers, and boots.

"I saw what happened out there," she said. "When did you and Carrington decide to work together?"

"Spur of the moment," Clint said. "He claimed he didn't want to see me gunned down by three cheap guns, but I think he just wanted to see my move before he made up his mind."

"Do you think he's going to challenge you?"

"He will, pretty soon."

"Then why not challenge him?"

"I've been thinking about that, too," Clint admitted.

"I hope you're not switching sides on me, Clint," Mary said.

"I've been on one side since I got here, Mary," he told her.

"And whose is that?"

"Mine."

"Well, I'm getting tired of staying in this room," she told him. "And I have a gun of my own."

"If you pick up a gun, Mary, you'll be out of your league," Clint said, "Do me a favor and just stay alive."

"I plan on staying alive, and in business," she told him.

"Good," Clint said. "Keep it that way."

As he turned to leave she asked, "And what are you planning to do?"

"I'm planning on going downstairs," he said, and left the room.

There were about half a dozen men in the saloon, and all of their eyes were on him as he came down. It occurred to him that some of the men might be Maitland's men. He was going to have to remain very aware.

He walked to the bar, kept six feet between himself and Carrington.

"More coffee?" Max asked him.

"Beer."

As Max set the beer in front of him, Carrington came walking over.

"What was on the lady's mind?" he asked.

"Staying alive, for one thing," Clint said. "Keeping this saloon, for another."

Carrington looked up at the second floor.

"So you're going to keep her in her room?"

"Yes."

"For how long?"

"As long as I can," Clint said. "At least until I find out what you're going to do."

Carrington laughed.

"I don't even know what I'm going to do," the gunman said. "But I'll tell you one thing I don't intend to do."

"What's that?"

"Kill a woman."

"That code of ethics, again?"

"You could call it that," Carrington said. "I don't kill women . . . not even for money."

Chapter Thirty-Seven

"Another beer?" Max asked Carrington.

"I don't think so," Carrington said. He looked at Clint, still standing six feet away. "How about a steak?"

"Sounds good," Clint said. "Where?"

"The Cattleman's Club."

"Maitland's table?"

"Yes."

"I appreciate the irony in that," Clint said.

Carrington put his empty mug down and said, "Let's go."

***

Clint and Carrington were met at the door.

"Hello, Mr. Carrington," the host greeted. "Will Mr. Maitland be joining you today?"

"No, not today," Carrington said. "Mr. Adams is going to eat with me."

"Very well," the man said. "Follow me, please."

They followed the man to a table near the back. For the most part the dining room was empty.

"I usually take a back table," Carrington said.

"I have the same habit."

A waiter came over and Carrington said, "Two steak dinners, and two mugs of beer."

"Yes, Sir."

The waiter returned quickly with the two beers.

"Thanks," Carrington said.

Two other tables were occupied, each by a single man. The two of them stared at Clint.

"Do you know who they are?" Clint asked.

"I know them, and they know me," Carrington said. "They're looking over here because they don't know you."

"Or because I'm not a member."

"They allow guests."

"Are you expecting your boss to come to town when he hears about the shooting?"

"Probably not," Carrington said. "But he might send some more men in. We'll have to wait and see."

"Men better with a gun than Dolan and the other two?" Clint asked.

"No," Carrington said, "but Maitland will send more than three, next time."

"So he'll deal in numbers, next time."

"I'm sure he will," Carrington said. "But this time he'll want to be sure I do something."

The waiter appeared, carrying two platters laden with steak and trimmings.

"Anything else, sir?" he asked.

"A basket of hot rolls would be nice," Carrington said.

"Comin' up."

As the waiter went back to the kitchen Clint and Carrington started on their steaks. The other two diners had already left.

"They don't wanna be here if there's any shootin'," Carrington said.

"Is there likely to be?" Clint asked.

"Not from me. Not while I'm eatin', anyway."

"You know what?" Clint asked. "I believe what you say about killing a woman."

"I appreciate that, Adams," Carrington said, "but tell me what else you believe—or what you don't believe."

"I don't believe you shot Andy Saxon in the back," Clint said, "and I don't believe you shot the man in the cell."

"So far you're two-for-two."

"Mary Ward says that someone fired a shot at her."

"I never heard anythin' about that," Carrington said. "If someone did that, it wasn't me."

"I believe that, too."

"You're startin' to make me think I'm an honest man."

"Not necessarily honest," Clint said, "but certainly honorable."

"When did you decide that?"

"When you put a bullet in Dolan's chest."

"I hate two-bit gunmen. They give men like you and me a bad name."

"Tell me, Carrington," Clint said, "are we still heading for a face-to-face in the streets?"

"Aren't you curious about which one of us is the best?" Carrington asked.

"No," Clint said.

"Why not?"

"Because we stood side-by-side, Del," Clint said. "I already know who's best, don't you?"

Chapter Thirty-Eight

When Clint and Carrington finished eating they left The Cattleman's Club together, stopping just outside.

"That was quite a meal," Clint said. "What's next for you?"

"I have to admit, my next move is not as clear as it was when I first got to town."

"How much do you really know about what Maitland is doing?" Clint asked.

"For the most part, when I'm working for someone, I only know what they want me to do."

"Is that the case with Maitland?"

"He's not as tough as he wants people to think," Carrington said. "He lets other people do his dirty work."

"Like killing Andy Saxon?"

"I didn't know Saxon," Carrington said, "but I'd heard of him. I never would've shot him in the back, no matter how much Maitland offered me. But Saxon was dead when I got here, so I don't really know if Maitland had anything to do with that."

"Was Dolan here when you signed on?"

"He was, so it could've been him. It's the kind of cowardly thing he and his two partners would've pulled."

"I'm glad it wasn't you. I don't see any reason for you and me to face off."

"I'm still not as sure about that as you are," Carrington said. "But I've had enough killin' for one day. I'll put my decision off until tomorrow."

"That suits me," Clint said. "Will you be staying in town?"

"They have rooms here for members," Carrington said. "I'll take Maitland's for the night."

"Then let's stay clear of each other while we're making up our minds," Clint said.

"Fine by me," Carrington said. "I'm startin' to like you too much to kill you."

"Yeah, I know what you mean," Clint said. "I'll see you tomorrow."

Clint strolled away from the Cattleman's Club, surprised at how safe he felt giving Carrington his back.

***

While the Gunsmith walked away Carrington watched for a few minutes, then turned and went inside to arrange for a room. He not only liked Clint Adams, he had a tremendous amount of respect for him. He was really going to hate it if he had to kill him.

***

Tom Finn had the dozen men picked out. Half of them were guns for hire. The other men would do just about anything for money.

Maitland addressed the first six in the barn, with the barn doors closed.

"What's Carrington doin'?" one of them asked.

"He's supposed to be taking care of the Gunsmith," Maitland said.

"And what if he doesn't?" a man named Weston asked.

"Then you fellas will have to take care of him, and the Gunsmith."

"And do you care how we do it?"

"I don't give a damn how it gets done, as long as it gets done."

The three men exchanged glances.

"Any problems?" Maitland asked.

"Well," Weston said, "none of us know Adams, or like Carrington, so I guess not."

"Is it just the six of us?" another man asked.

"I've got six others lined up," Maitland said. "They're not guns for hire, but they'll do anything for money."

"Seems to me twelve men is plenty, even if six of them ain't pros," Weston said. "But we're pros."

"Don't worry about that," Maitland said, "You six will be paid like pros."

"When do we go to town?" Weston asked.

"Tomorrow morning," Maitland said. "I'm going to want this to be over by tomorrow night."

"And what about the other six men?" Weston asked.

"I'm going to talk with them in the house when I leave here. Weston, when you all get to town, you'll be in charge." Maitland looked at the other men. "Any problem with that?"

They all shook their heads.

"All right," Maitland said, "after I've talked to the others I'll send them over here. They'll know that you're in charge."

"Yes, sir."

"I'll talk to you again in the morning, Weston, before you all leave for town."

"Are we gonna just ride right in?" Weston asked.

"Right down Trail Street," Maitland said. "No need to hide."

"All right."

"I'll see you all tomorrow."

He left the barn and walked to the house. Tom Finn was waiting on the porch.

"Good, you're here," Maitland said.

"You told me to be here."

"Yes, yes, I did. Come inside with me."

They entered the house together. The six men in the front room came to attention.

"Just wait there, boys," Maitland said. "Come on, Finn."

The foreman followed his boss down the hall. Maitland seated himself behind his desk.

"You been wanting a more active role in my business, haven't you, Tom?"

"Well, yeah, boss, but . . . what'd you have in mind?"

"You used to be pretty good with a gun, didn't you?"

"You know I was."

"In fact, you thought you were the best there ever was," Maitland said.

"Well, yeah, but I put my guns away a long time ago, you know that."

"But can you still shoot?"

"Of course," Finn said. "You don't forget that."

"When's the last time you used a gun?"

"Well . . . I take my gun out and shoot, on occasion. But I haven't fired at a man in years."

"Okay, Tom," Maitland said, "this is what I want you to do . . ."

Chapter Thirty-Nine

In the morning Clint woke, somehow feeling that things were going to come to a boil that day. He went downstairs to have breakfast in the hotel dining room. When he got to the doorway, he saw Carrington seated at the table he usually sat at.

Newly met him at the door.

"That fella said you wouldn't mind if he sat at your table."

"It's all right, Newly. Has he ordered, yet?"

"Just coffee."

"Bring us both some ham-and-eggs, too."

"Yes sir."

Newly went to the kitchen, and Clint went over and joined Carrington.

"I hope you don't mind," Carrington said. "I figured you were like me, and you'd have a regular table."

"It's fine," Clint said. "How'd you sleep at The Cattleman's Club?"

"Like the dead. Woke up starvin'."

"So did I."

As if on cue, Newly appeared with their plates. The slabs of ham were as thick as steaks and he followed quickly with a basket of warm rolls. This whole situation reminded Clint of a recent experience with a bunch of town tamers. When this was finally over, he was going to treat himself to a very different kind of experience.

"What's on your mind?" Carrington asked him.

"Huh? Oh, I'm thinking after this I might spend some time minding my own business."

"I guess that'll depend on how this all ends, huh?" Carrington said.

"I think it's going to depend on you and your boss," Clint said.

"I know what Maitland wants," Carrington said. "I'm just waitin' to figure out what I want."

"You said you didn't know much about Maitland's business."

"Well, I know he wants The Blue Bonnet," the gunman said, "and I know he wants me to take care of you."

"Then with me out of his way, he can move on with whatever his plans are for his ranch, and the town." Clint shook his head. "This would have gone much smoother if Bent Fork had a legitimate lawman."

"That's true. Richards only does what Maitland tells him to."

"Is he that far under his thumb?" Clint asked.

"Completely."

"So far that he might've killed that man in his cell?" Clint asked.

"I don't think Maitland would've trusted that to Richards."

"Then who?"

"Anybody on his payroll."

"The foreman?"

"Finn? I don't think so. He seems to be strictly a ranch foreman."

"That's been the impression I've gotten when I've seen him."

"All Maitland had to do was point one of his lesser guns."

"Backshooters"

"If that's what he wants them to do, sure."

"Del," Clint said, "I want the man who shot Andy Saxon."

"That man was just a gun, Clint," Carrington said. "Maitland's the one who pointed it."

"Can you prove that?" Clint asked. "Would you testify to that?"

"I'm not very good in court or working with the law. I have to stick to what I'm good at."

"And I know what that is," Clint said.

"It's what we're both good at," Carrington said. "But who's better? That's still something to find out."

"When Maitland calls the play," Clint said.

"I told you, I'm on my own," Carrington corrected him.

"I guess we'll just have to wait and see," Clint said.

They left the dining room and stepped outside.

"What's on your schedule?" Clint asked.

"Up to now, not much, but look," Carrington said, inclining his head.

Clint looked down Trail Street and saw twelve men riding in. This really was starting to resemble his recent interaction with the Town Tamers. That had turned into a blood bath.

"You know them?" Clint asked.

"Oh, yeah," Carrington said. "They work for Maitland."

"All of them?"

"Yeah," Carrington said. "That one in front is Weston. He and half of them are money guns. The others are just hands, but Maitland's obviously gonna start dealin' in numbers."

"Do you know them well?"

"I didn't mix with them, but we know each other."

"Are they good?" Clint asked.

"Better than Dolan, but not by much."

"So I only need to worry if they come for me all at once," Clint said.

"Well, you can count on one thing, then," Carrington said.

"What's that?"

"You won't be gettin' shot in the back."

Chapter Forty

While they watched, the twelve men rode to the Lucky Lady Saloon and dismounted in front. They all looked up and down Trail Street before going in. The man Carrington identified as Weston went in last after a final look.

"Weston saw you," Clint said.

"Yeah, he did."

"So what now?"

"I don't think they'll do anythin' until I do," Carrington said. "Or you do."

"You want to play a waiting game?" Clint asked.

"I have been," Carrington said, "but I'm really not very good at it."

"So I guess we'll go have a beer," Clint said.

Carrington grinned and said, lead the way."

They stepped into the street and headed for the Lucky Lady.

***

As they entered, they saw all the Maitland men lined up at the bar. Weston raised his glass in a salute to Carrington, who led Clint to the bar.

"Two beers," he said.

The bartender recognized all of the men as working for Maitland, especially Carrington. But he hesitated before giving Clint a beer.

"He's with me," the gunman told him.

"Whatever you say," the bartender said, and set one in front of Clint.

"Hey, Weston," Carrington said, "join us at a table."

"Oh, sure," Weston said, and walked across the room with Carrington and Clint. They sat while the other men watched with interest.

"I'm not gonna ask what you're doin' in town," Carrington said. "I'm sure Maitland sent you all because of what happened to Dolan and the others."

"You and Adams killed them," Weston said. "Why'd you do that?"

"Dolan and his partners were gonna go against Adams three-to-one. He deserved better than that."

"He deserves whatever the boss says he deserves," Weston said, then looked at Clint and added, "No offense."

"None taken," Clint said. "You're working for the man."

"Still," Carrington said, "twelve against one is even worse. Any man deserves better than that."

"We got our orders, Carrington," Weston said. "If you don't get the job done, we will."

Carrington looked past Weston at the men at the bar.

"I see five guns with you, and six cowpokes," he commented. "How do you feel about your chances? I mean, this is the Gunsmith we're talkin' about."

"I think we got enough guns to get the job done," Weston said.

"And what if it's twelve to two?"

"Why would you stand with him against those odds?" Weston asked.

"Because I wouldn't stand by and watch you all gun him down," Carrington said.

Weston shrugged and said, "Still good odds."

"Maybe," Carrington said, "but one of us would kill you first. After that you're out of the play, and the odds change."

Weston licked his lips nervously and took a sip of his beer to wet them further.

"Give your decision some thought, Weston," Carrington said. "Talk to your men."

"That's good advice," Clint added.

Weston licked his lips again, then left the table with his beer and went back to the bar.

"You know," Clint said, "if they all drew now and started firing, we'd be in trouble."

"They won't."

"What makes you so sure?"

"Their orders are to wait and see what I do," Carrington said. "Also, Weston's nervous, and he'll pass those nerves on to the others."

"You can put all this to rest by killing me," Clint said.

"Oh, believe me, I'm considering that," Carrington said, "but you ain't just gonna sit there and let me do that."

"No, not likely."

"What would you like to do?"

"Well, I'd like to avoid a blood bath."

"Then I have a suggestion," Carrington said.

"What's that?"

"Let's leave Weston and his men here and go out to the ranch to see Maitland."

"Are you saying he has no guns out there now?"

"As far as I can see," Carrington said, "they're all here. All he's gonna have out there are some cowhands, and his foreman."

"You think I'll be able to get the truth out of him?" Clint asked.

"I think we all want to get this business over with."

"Suits me," Clint said, "Let's go."

Chapter Forty-One

Clint thought that bracing Maitland at his ranch while his guns were in town was a good idea. But, of course, he still had to keep a sharp eye on Carrington.

They left the saloon in a leisurely manner, so as not to show any urgency to Weston and the others. Once outside, with no one following them, they went to the livery and claimed their horses. They avoided Trail Street and left town without being seen.

Or so they thought . . .

***

A man named Gillis was standing at the bar, drinking a beer and looking out the window. He decided to go out and walk Trail Street, to see where Carrington and Adams had gone. It was then he saw them ride out of the livery stable, virtually sneaking out of town. He hurried back to the Lucky Lady . . .

***

As they approached the ranch in the late afternoon, they saw no one at the corral, or anywhere else on the grounds. There was no sign of Finn, the foreman, who made a habit of greeting visitors.

"It's pretty deserted," Clint said.

"He should still have some cowhands here," Carrington said. "And Finn, the foreman."

"Then he's hiding them," Clint said.

"If we had guns trained on us right now, I'd feel it. Wouldn't you?"

"Definitely."

They rode to the base of the front steps and dismounted. They looked around before climbing the steps and approaching the front door.

"Knock?" Carrington said.

"Let's just walk in," Clint suggested.

"Get under Maitland's skin right away, huh?"

Carrington tried the door, found it unlocked and opened it. They entered, unchallenged, and stood just inside.

"Maitland!" Carrington shouted.

There was no answer.

They looked into the front room and found it empty.

"Let's try his office," Carrington said. "Down the hall."

They walked down the hall quietly, but as they approached the door they heard horses outside—many horses.

"They're back?" Clint said.

"Maybe we didn't slip out of town as easily as we thought," Carrington said. "Let's take a quick look in his office."

They hurried down the hall to the office, looked in and found it empty.

"I don't get this," Carrington said.

"Could there be other riders out front, and not the ones from town?" Clint asked.

"It's possible," Carrington said. "Maybe we should go out the back."

"Our horses are out front, so they know we're here."

"That's right. Then we might as well go out and face them, whoever they are."

"Let's go."

They made their way to the front door, then stopped.

"Let's take a look out the front window first," Clint said.

They moved to the window and looked out together.

"Yep, that's Weston and the boys, all right."

"We go out the front door we're taking a chance they'll open fire," Clint said.

"And riddle the boss's house with bullets? I don't think so. If anything, they'd want us down off the porch. Let's try it."

"You know, Del, I think you're addicted to taking chances. That's why you decided to talk with me and stand with me."

"I told you, I wanted to see if you were still the Gunsmith."

Chapter Forty-Two

They stepped out the front door and stopped. All twelve men were still mounted, their horses in a semicircle around Carrington and Clint.

"I thought you boys were in town," Carrington said.

"We thought you were there, too," Weston said, "until Gillis spotted you ridin' out."

"Sneakin' out," Gillis said.

"We just thought we'd pay Mr. Maitland a visit," Carrington said. "He probably wouldn't like seein' you all back here."

"Then maybe we all better leave," Weston suggested.

"By the way," Carrington said, "do you know where the boss is?"

"No," Weston said, "he was here when we left this morning."

He turned and looked at his men. "Let's get back to town."

He wheeled his horse around and led them all away. In minutes, Clint and Carrington were standing there alone, relieved that no one had overreacted.

They walked down the steps, mounted up and rode back to town.

***

Clint and Carrington left their horses in the livery, then walked out.

"Where to?" Carrington asked.

"Well, either The Blue Bonnet or my hotel. What about you?"

"I'm curious if Maitland is at The Cattleman's Club."

"Wouldn't we have passed each other along the way?"

"Not if he was already in town," Carrington said. "He could be in an office in The Lucky Lady, since he owns it."

"That's true."

"Let's try there," Carrington suggested.

"The whole crew might be back there."

"Well, they haven't done anything rash, yet."

"So you want to push some more."

"A bit," Carrington said. "Let's see what happens."

They headed for The Lucky Lady.

"What about your fee, Del?" Clint asked. "Are you giving that up?"

"If I get the job done," Carrington said, "I'll get paid."

***

Tom Finn entered Maitland's office finn in the back of The Lucky Lady.

"They're on their way here, boss."

"Were they out at the house?"

"Yes, and all the men went there."

"And?"

"And they all came back."

Maitland sat back in his chair.

"I'm tired of people thinking I killed Andy Saxon," he said. "I want this to be over with today."

Finn touched the gun on his hip and said, "So you want me to act?"

"I do."

"And you'll pay me what we agreed on?"

"Oh yes. Every cent we agreed on. You get this done, Tom, you'll be a rich man."

Finn touched the gun on his hip again.

"Can you do it, Tom?" Maitland asked.

"I can do it," Finn said, "but which one? Carrington or Adams?"

"Let's see how it goes," Maitland said, "Whichever one you kill, it'll be a fair fight. Then Weston and the rest will kill the other one." Maitland stood up, "Let's go out and sit at a table."

Maitland stood and walked ahead of Finn.

***

As Clint and Carrington entered The Lucky Lady, they saw Maitland coming out a door in the back, followed by Finn.

"Why is Finn wearing a gun?" Clint asked. "I thought he was just the foreman."

"I don't know," Carrington said. "I've never seen him wearing a gun, before."

"Does Maitland want that many guns that he put one on his foreman?" Clint asked.

"I guess we'll find out," Carrington said. "It looks like we're all here."

Maitland and Finn sat at a table and a saloon girl brought them each a beer.

"Let's get a beer each and join them," Carrington said. "Maybe we can find out just what's goin' on."

Clint nodded and they both walked to the bar. Several of Maitland's men stepped aside to give them room. They collected two beers from the bartender, then carried them over to Maitland's table.

"Mind if we sit down?" Clint asked.

"Not at all," Maitland said. "I was hoping we'd find out what was going on."

"That's funny," Carrington said. "We were just sayin' the same thing."

Chapter Forty-Three

"It seems you have taken up with the Gunsmith, Carrington," Maitland observed.

"Well, you seem to have sent a lot of men to town," Carrington said. "Did you think I needed that much back-up?"

"After I heard what you did to Dolan and the others, I had to wonder if you'd changed sides."

"I've always been on my side," Carrington said.

"I wish I had known that sooner," Maitland said. "Don't you, Adams?"

"I've been waiting to find out a lot of things, Maitland," Clint said. "Like which of your men you had backshoot Andy Saxon."

"I'm sorry to disappoint you, Adams, but that wasn't my doing. All I did with Saxon was buy his ranch."

"So who killed him, or had him killed?"

"If I knew that I would've told you much sooner, if only to get rid of you."

"And the killer with the drummer's case?" Clint asked.

"I'm going to lay it on the table, Adams," Maitland said. "That *was* my doing."

"And killing him in his cell?"

"You should talk to Sheriff Richards about that," Maitland said. "I paid him to take care of that."

Clint studied the man. Why admit to hiring Luftin, and then having him killed, and yet still lie about Andy Saxon?

"So who killed Saxon?" Clint asked.

"I don't know," Maitland said. "I assume it was somebody who hated him."

Clint was starting to believe Maitland hadn't killed Andy Saxon. If that was true, then who did?

"If you didn't kill Andy," Clint said, "then there's no reason for us to go up against each other."

"That depends," Maitland said. "What if Mary Ward asks for your help?"

"She has," Clint said, "but she's still convinced you killed Saxon, and that you want to kill her."

"I admit I want her place," Maitland said, "but not bad enough to kill her."

"Then who took a shot at her?"

"I don't have the slightest idea."

"Maybe we should find out who did, before we start shooting at each other."

"I don't know, Adams," Maitland said. "Shooting is what you and Carrington are known for."

"You've got plenty of shooters here yourself, Maitland," Carrington said. "Are you dying to turn them loose?"

"They're just available if I need them."

Carrington looked at the foreman.

"And what are you doin' wearin' a gun, Finn?" he asked.

"Just like the rest of the boys," Finn said. "I'm just bein' available."

"I've never seen you with a gun before," Carrington said. "Can you handle it?"

"I can handle it. I just haven't had to for a long time."

"That's interestin'," Carrington said, "Why not show us?"

"Whataya mean?" Finn asked. "You want me to draw on you?"

"No, I'm not callin' you out, but let's see what you got." Carrington called a saloon girl over. "Four glasses."

"Whiskey?"

"No," Carrington said, "just four empty glasses."

"Yes, Sir."

She hurried to the bar and came back with four shot glasses.

"Watch," Carrington said. He took an empty glass, tossed it into the air, then drew and fired. The glass shattered and the saloon went quiet as everyone turned to see what was going on. Carrington picked up another glass and said, "Now you."

Finn looked at Maitland.

"Go ahead," the rancher said.

"I'm not a good target shooter," Finn said.

"Give it a try," Carrington said, and tossed the glass. It flew into the air and fell to the floor.

"I wasn't ready," Finn said.

"You've always gotta be ready, Finn."

"Hey," Maitland said, "I'm not paying anybody to shoot at glasses."

"I was just checkin' your man out, Maitland."

"I'm kind of tired of you, Carrington," Maitland said. "I don't feel it's in my best interest to keep you employed."

"In other words?"

"In other words, you're fired."

"You owe me money for the time I've been here."

"I don't think so," Maitland said. "So far all you've done is kill some of my men."

"Well, there are plenty more here to pick from," Carrington said, looking around. "It might just be easier for you to pay me."

"Maybe," Maitland said, "if you get by Finn, I'll consider it."

"Finn?" Carrington asked. "You've got guns for hire here, and you want me to get by your foreman?"

Maitland said, "Let's start there and see where we go."

Chapter Forty-Four

"In here?" Carrington asked.

"On the street," Maitland said. "We don't want any-one getting hit by a stray bullet."

"Suits me," Carrington said, standing up.

"This isn't really necessary," Clint said.

"You don't even have to come out," Carrington said. He turned and went out the batwing doors.

Finn looked at Maitland, who nodded. The foreman stood up and followed Carrington out. Clint decided he had to see this, so he stood and walked to the front window.

"What do you think?" Maitland asked, coming up alongside him.

"Carrington's fast," Clint said. "I don't know any-thing about your foreman."

"As a young man he was a fast gun," Maitland said. "Fastest I ever saw, but then he put the gun down. I hired him because he's reliable, made him my foreman when I bought the place from Saxon."

"And he hasn't picked up his gun since?" Clint asked.

"No," Maitland said, "but he insists it's not something you forget. When it looked like Carrington was aligning himself with you, I told him to strap it on."

"And you think he'll take Carrington?"

"He says he will," Maitland said. "He claims he's as fast as ever."

"You can call it off now, Maitland," Clint said.

"If I do will you leave town?"

"One's got nothing to do with the other," Clint insisted.

"We'll see about that," Maitland said.

Some of the other men moved away from the bar to take a look.

Outside, on the street, the two men faced off . . .

***

As the men moved to the center of the street bystanders ran for cover from which they would be able to watch.

"You sure you want to do this, Finn?"

"Mr. Maitland wants me to," Finn said, "I owe him."

"Enough to die for him?"

"Mr. Carrington," Finn said, "I'm very fast."

"It didn't seem that way inside."

"I don't shoot at glasses."

"All right, then," Carrington said, "Make your move."

The words were barely out of Carrington's mouth when Finn drew and fired before the other man could even twitch. The bullet struck Carrington dead center in the chest. It happened so fast he barely felt the bullet punch into him. He had time to say, "Jesus—" before he fell onto his face in the street, dead.

***

Clint was shocked by the speed of Finn's draw and ran out the batwing doors as Carrington hit the ground. Maitland simply turned and walked back to his table.

When Clint reached Carrington, he leaned over him to check and see if he was dead.

Tom Finn came over, holstered his gun and looked down at the dead man.

"I told him I was fast," he said, then turned and went back into the saloon.

Clint stared at the man, then turned as Sheriff Richards approached.

"Did you do this?" he asked Clint.

"No," Clint said, "it was Tom Finn."

"What? The foreman?"

"Apparently," Clint said, "he has a past."

"I'll get some men to move the body," Richards said.

"After that you better leave town," Clint said.

"What?"

"Maitland gave you up for shooting your prisoner," Clint said. "I don't have time to deal with you, but I'll be sending for a federal lawman to handle it—"

"But, wait—"

". . . not to mention a circuit judge."

"But Adams, wait—"

Clint turned and went back into The Lucky Lady. He stopped just inside the batwing doors and while everyone looked at him, he locked eyes with Maitland.

"What did I tell you?" the rancher asked.

Tom Finn was sitting with his back to the door, and did not turn around.

"I guess that leaves you standing alone, Adams," Maitland said. "Whether you believe I had Saxon killed or not, I think you'd be better off leaving town."

"Or what, you'll let all your men loose on me, or just Finn?" Clint asked.

"I guess I'll leave that up to you," Maitland said. "You just saw what Finn can do."

"Isn't this all a little bit of overkill, Maitland?" Clint asked. "Send your men home and lets you and me work this out."

"There's nothing to work out, Adams," Maitland said. "I want everything I want, and that's that. Now that Carrington's dead, you're all alone."

"Then turn your men loose, Maitland, because you'll be the first one I kill."

"Finn will kill you, Adams, whether they all start firing, or you face him."

"You're going to need a new lawman. I sent Richards packing."

"I'll be restocking this town with people once you're gone, Adams. And that includes the lady at the Blue Bonnet."

"And will that be without killing her?"

"I don't hire men who kill women," Maitland said. "I'll buy her out eventually, like I did Saxon."

"And you still say you didn't kill Saxon."

"I didn't kill him or have him killed," Maitland said. "But Carrington's dead and the only one I see being killed next is you, Adams, if you don't ride out."

"Whatever happens, Maitland, when I have a Federal Marshal ride in here, you and your men will be behind bars. Even if I'm not here to see it."

"That's been tried, Adams. The Feds aren't sending anybody in here."

"I have a personal friend who's a marshal," Clint said. "He'll be here." He was referring to Custis Long, also known as Longarm.

"You're bluffing," Maitland said. "I'm the law here."

"Your sheriff is done," Clint said. "You won't be able to buy the federal law. You and your men will be going to jail."

A concerned look came over the faces of half Maitland's men—the ones who were not paid gunmen.

"You might as well let your cowhands go home," Clint said.

Maitland didn't say a word, but Weston spoke to the men in low tone, and half of them walked past Clint and out of the saloon.

"I assume the rest of the men here are money guns, Maitland. I hope you're paying them enough to go to jail."

Weston turned and spoke to the rest of the men, and they also walked past Clint and out the door. Weston and Finn were the only two left. The rest of the men in the saloon were just patrons.

"What's going on, Weston?" Maitland demanded.

"We saw what you just did to Carrington, Mr. Maitland. If Adams is telling the truth, none of us want to go to jail, and sure as hell none of us wanna die, like Carrington."

"Go on, then, Weston," Maitland said. "Get out with the rest. You're all fired."

"That suits us, Mr. Maitland. This is all gettin' outta hand, anyway."

Weston left without looking at Clint.

"That leaves you and Finn, Maitland," Clint said. "You want to stand up?"

"I should have done this the moment you rode in, Adams," Maitland said. "Finn will take you. In here or on the street?"

"Right here's fine," Clint said. "I'm not looking to put on a show."

Maitland looked at Finn and nodded. The foreman stood up and turned to face Clint.

"You don't want to do this, kid," Clint said.

"I do what Mr. Maitland tells me," Finn said. "You'd be smart to do the same thing."

"If I was smart I would've left here days ago," Clint said. "Come on, let's get this over with."

Finn didn't hesitate. He went for his gun, moving like lightning. He actually cleared leather when Clint shot him in the chest. Clint didn't hesitate after that. He turned as Weston came through the batwing doors, gun in hand, and shot him between the eyes. As Weston hit the floor Clint turned back to Maitland, who was frozen in place.

"I could kill you now, Maitland, or leave you for the federal marshal. What do you say?"

"I think I'll take my chances with the law."

"Then you better walk out," Clint said. "But with your lawman out of the picture, you better have your dead men moved to the undertaker."

"Right, right."

Maitland moved past Clint and stepped over Weston's body.

"And you better find a buyer for this place, and the ranch."

"My ranch?"

"Andy Saxon's ranch."

Maitland stared at Clint, then said, "Right," and left.

Clint gave Maitland time to get to the undertaker, then left The Lucky Lady himself. He went to the telegraph office and sent that message to Custis Long, in Denver.

The one he had bluffed Maitland about.

Chapter Forty-Five

Clint sent the telegram, told the clerk to bring the response to the hotel.

"If I'm not there give it to a waiter named Newly," he instructed.

"I know Newly," the clerk said.

"What's your name?"

"Hector."

"Okay, Hector, bring it over as soon as you get the answer."

"Yes, Sir."

Clint left the telegraph office. He walked down Trail Street until he got to the point where Andy had been shot. He stopped, looked around and it hit him like a pole axe. He walked to The Blue Bonnet and went inside. There were only a few customers, and Max looking bored behind the bar. He stood up straight as Clint approached the bar.

"Beer?" Max asked.

"Yeah."

Max set it in front of him.

"I heard the shots," he said.

"It's all over."

"Maitland's dead?"

"No, but his money guns are, and the rest of his men left. There'll be a federal marshal here in a few days. He'll arrest Maitland if he's still here."

"That's good. So he killed Andy?"

"No," Clint said. "You know who killed Andy, Max. I should've figured it out as soon as I saw the windows upstairs. There was no other vantage point for somebody to have shot Andy in the back."

"Mr. Adams—"

"When Marshal Long gets here, he'll arrest Mary, too."

"Mr. Adams, she went crazy when Andy said he wasn't going to marry her. When I heard the shot, I ran upstairs and found her by the window. I took the rifle from her and walked her to her room. I—I think she still doesn't remember doin' it."

"You can talk to the marshal when he gets here and see if you can convince him."

"And what are you gonna do?"

"I'm leaving."

"Will you say goodbye to her?"

"I don't want to see her." He turned to leave.

"She might go crazy again!" Max said. "What do I do?"

"Do me a favor," Clint said, "see that she doesn't shoot me in the back on my way out of town."

He left and walked to the telegraph office to send one more.

Upcoming New Release!

THE GUNSMITH

INVITATION TO A BANK ROBBERY
BOOK 491

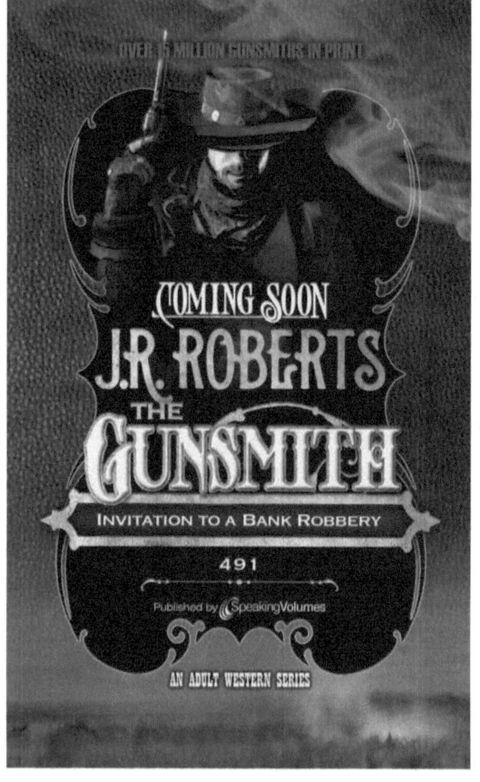

**For more information
visit: www.SpeakingVolumes.us**

Now Available!

THE GUNSMITH SERIES
BOOKS 430 – 489

For more information
visit: www.SpeakingVolumes.us

Now Available!

THE GUNSMITH GIANT SERIES

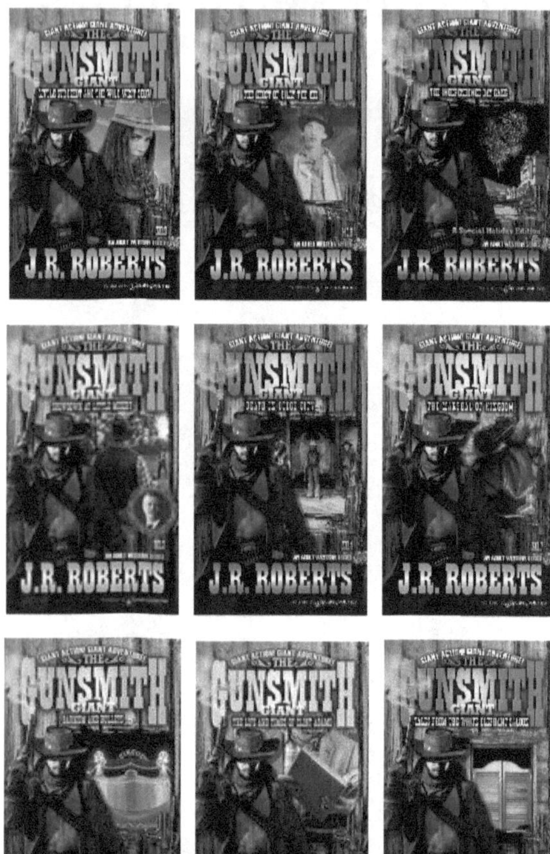

For more information
visit: www.SpeakingVolumes.us

Now Available!

LADY GUNSMITH SERIES
BOOKS 1 - 10

AND OUR
HOLIDAY SPECIAL EDITION
ROCKY DOYLE AND THE CHRISTMAS GIFT

For more information
visit: www.SpeakingVolumes.us

Now Available!

ROBERT J. RANDISI'S
RAT PACK MYSTERIES

GET SWEPT AWAY INTO
THE LAS VEGAS ERA OF THE 60s

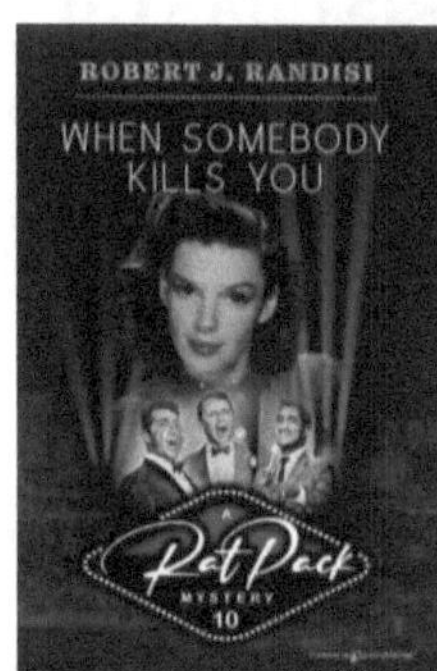

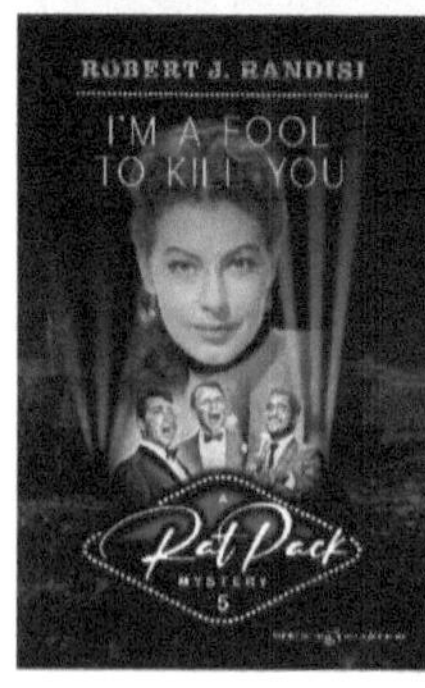

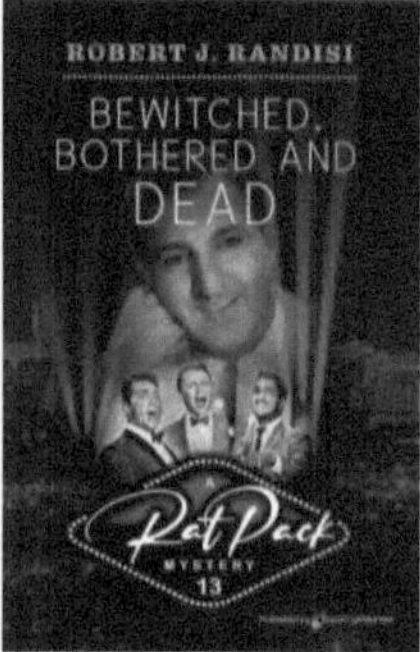

For more information
visit: www.SpeakingVolumes.us

Now Available!

AWARD-WINNING AUTHOR
ROBERT J. RANDISI (J.R. ROBERTS)

For more information
visit: www.SpeakingVolumes.us

Now Available!

AWARD-WINNING AUTHOR
ROBERT J. RANDISI
TALBOT ROPER NOVELS

For more information
visit: www.SpeakingVolumes.us

www.ingramcontent.com/pod-product-compliance
Lightning Source LLC
Chambersburg PA
CBHW051233130726
47988CB00001B/327